Flock

First Nations Stories Then and Now

Edited by
Ellen van Neerven

UQP

First published 2021 by University of Queensland Press
PO Box 6042, St Lucia, Queensland 4067 Australia
Reprinted 2021 (twice)

University of Queensland Press (UQP) acknowledges the Traditional Owners and their
custodianship of the lands on which UQP operates. We pay our respects to their Ancestors
and their descendants, who continue cultural and spiritual connections to Country.
We recognise their valuable contributions to Australian and global society.

uqp.com.au
reception@uqp.com.au

Cover design by Josh Durham (Design by Committee)
Cover artwork *Redtails Looking for Shelter* by Kukula Mcdonald
Author photograph by Anna Jacobson
Typeset in 12/17 pt Bembo Std by Post Pre-press Group, Brisbane
Printed in Australia by McPherson's Printing Group

 Cover artwork courtesy of Bindi Mwerre Anthurre Artists
(Lifestyle Solutions Pty Ltd). This image embodies traditional
knowledge of the Luritja community. It was created with the
consent of the custodians of the community.

 This project is supported by the Copyright Agency's
Cultural Fund.

 University of Queensland Press is supported by the
Queensland Government through Arts Queensland.

  University of Queensland Press is assisted by the
Australian Government through the Australia
Council, its arts funding and advisory body.

A catalogue record for this book is available from the National Library of Australia

ISBN 978 0 7022 6303 3 (pbk)
ISBN 978 0 7022 6458 0 (epdf)
ISBN 978 0 7022 6459 7 (epub)
ISBN 978 0 7022 6460 3 (kindle)

University of Queensland Press uses papers that are natural, renewable and recyclable
products made from wood grown in well-managed forests and other controlled sources.
The logging and manufacturing processes conform to the environmental regulations of the
country of origin.

Contents

Introduction

As I write, the brush turkey is making a nest outside the window, scratching the earth, gathering leaves, to the beat of my typing. I kneel on the lounge to look through the window and I don't see the bird, because it's underneath me. I don't see the bird, but I hear the bird.

I am writing on unceded Yagera and Turrbal dhagan. I acknowledge the First Nations of all of the contributors in this book, including my own Yugambeh Nation. This collection's stories are organised by author, in descending alphabetical order. There are nineteen stories by nineteen writers plus a story of mine, as an offering.

All the stories gathered in *Flock* have been previously published or presented. The span of publication ranges from 1996 to 2021: twenty-five years, though the roots of these First Nations stories span generations, this book being part of a much bigger conversation. Many collections have come before this one, too many to mention. Many a gathering of stories has occurred on this continent since time immemorial. We owe a great deal to our literary Elders who have come before us.

For me the title perfectly fits the collection. Contributor Bryan Andy called it the 'most affirming title ever', when I first emailed him about this book. The title is, in part, inspired by *Flock* contributor Jeanine Leane's tribute to our beloved Kuracca Kerry Reed-Gilbert who we lost in 2019. Jeanine's obituary, published in *Overland* magazine, goes as follows:

> *Like the kuracca, that is a sentinel bird – always watching over the rest of the mob, Aunty Kerry nurtured, encouraged and inspired a generation of writers.*

I am reminded of how Aunty KRG brought us together under the banner of the First Nations Australian Writers Network, of which she was a co-founder and the inaugural chair. In August 2018, in what was to be her last year as FNAWN chairperson, Aunty convened a large diverse gathering of First Nations writers in Canberra from all states and territories.

Jeanine's tribute continues:

> *On the morning that she passed, a mob of kuracca flew in, dipping low in a thick cloud over her old home, calling her passing across the sky, taking her spirit home. Vale Kuracca, Aunty Kerry Reed-Gilbert, as you fly high and safe on the journey back to your Dreaming. Under your wings is the strength of us as Black writers.*

When I hear the distinctive sharp yelp-caw sound of the kuracca (sulphur-crested cockatoo in the Wiradjuri language, geira in mine) flying overhead, I see Aunty watching over us. I know she would have been incredibly proud of this collection.

A painting by Kukula Mcdonald features on the cover of this book. I've been wearing Kukula Mcdonald's *Red-Tailed Black Cockatoo* print on a black T-shirt for many years now. Mum bought it for me as a present from Papunya when she was living in Alice Springs and I loved it from the moment I saw it. Admittedly, the tee is a bit tight on me compared to what it used to be, but I still wear it often. The brushstrokes and colours on the solid black material are often remarked upon, particularly by mob.

Kukala's artwork immediately came to mind when we started to think about covers for this book and what the book represents. I am thrilled we can feature Kukula's mob of redtails on the cover; for me, it symbolises what this book is about. We all have our own pair of beautiful wings, but we fly together in formation. Together we are stronger. We flock together.

The process of choosing the works for this collection took several months. Yasmin Smith was an incredible editorial assistant. And my mum, Maria van Neerven-Currie, was an important sounding board. The stories come from single-authored short story collections as well as literary journals and previous anthologies. Archie Weller's story was first published in the important *Australian Short Stories*, a journal started up by Bruce Pascoe and Lyn Harwood. Jeanine Leane's story was published in a special cross-cultural 2014 edition of Māori literary journal *Ora Nui*, edited by Anton Black and Aunty Kerry Reed-Gilbert. The opening story, 'Cloud Busting', comes from Tara June Winch's groundbreaking debut, *Swallow the Air* (2006), which won the David Unaipon Award and launched her career. The final story, Bryan Andy's 'Moama', was performed at the Bogong Moth Storytelling night at the Blak & Bright Festival directed by Jane Harrison in 2019.

The writers in this collection are well-known and award-winning, as well as emerging and new. Their stories span generations, geographies and genres. Some are touching, some gritty, some funny, many are all three. Some contributors write from autobiographical experiences, others do not. Short stories are a specific type of writing that requires precision of language and the right mix of narrative elements. A good short story will have been laboured over by the writer and is a gift to the reader. We have selected a diverse range of stories that showcase the art of a good short story, as well as being strong monuments to First Nations pasts, presents and futures.

Cloud Busting

Tara June Winch

Tara June Winch is a Wiradjuri writer based in France. She has written essays, short fiction and memoir for *Vogue*, *Vice*, *McSweeneys* and various other publications. Her first novel, *Swallow the Air*, won the 2006 David Unaipon Award and was followed by a collection of stories, *After the Carnage*. She won the 2020 Miles Franklin Literary Award for her 2019 novel, *The Yield*.

We go cloud busting, Billy and me, down at the beach, belly up to the big sky. We make rainbows that pour out from our heads, squinting our eyes into the gathering. Fairy-flossed pincushion clouds explode. We hold each other's hand; squeeze really hard to build up the biggest brightest rainbow and *Bang!* Shoot it up to the sky, bursting cloud suds that scatter, escaping into the air alive.

We toss our bodies off the eelgrass-covered dunes and race down to the shore where seaweed beads trace the waterline. Little bronze teardrops – we bust them too. Bubble-wrapped pennies.

We collect pipis, squirming our heels into the shallow water, digging deeper under the sandy foam. Reaching down for our prize, we find lantern shells, cockles, and sometimes periwinkles, bleached white. We snatch them up, filling our pockets. We find shark egg capsules like dried-out leather corkscrews and cuttlebones and sand snail skeletons, and branches, petrified to stone. We find sherbet-coloured coral clumps, sponge tentacles and sea mats, and bluebottles – we bust them with a stick. We find weed-ringlet doll wigs and strings of brown pearls; I wear them as bracelets. We get drunk on the salt air and laughter.

We dance, wiggling our bottoms from the dunes' height. We crash into the surf, we swim, we dive, and we tumble. We empty our lungs and weigh ourselves cross-legged to the seabed. There we have tea parties underwater. Quickly, before we swim up for mouthfuls of air.

I'm not scared of the ocean, that doesn't come until later. When we're kids we have no fear – it gets sucked out in the rips. We swim with the current, like breeding turtles and hidden jellyfish, as we drift out onto the shore.

We climb the dunes again, covered in sticky sand and sea gifts. We ride home and string up dry sea urchins at our window. We break open our pipis and Mum places each half under the grill or fries them in the saucepan, with onion and tomatoes. We empty our pockets and line the seashells along the windowsill. Mum starts on about the saucepans; she wants to tell us stories even though we know most of them off by heart, over and over, every detail. The saucepans, she says, the best bloody saucepans.

Billy and me sit at the window, watching Mum while she fries and begins. I'm still busting clouds through the kitchen pane, as they pass over the roof guttering and burst quietly in my rainbow.

'It was Goulburn, 1967,' Mum would begin.

'Where's that?' we'd say.

'Somewhere far away, a Goulburn that doesn't exist anymore,' she'd answer and carry on with her story.

Anyway, Goulburn, '67. All my brothers and sisters had been put into missions by then, except Fred who went and lived with my mother's sister. And me, I was with my mother, probably cos my skin's real dark, see – but that's another story, you don't need to know that. So old Mum and me were sent to Goulburn from the river, to live in these little flats. Tiny things, flatettes or something. Mum was working for a real nice family, at the house cooking and cleaning; they were so nice to Mum. I would go to work with her, used to sit outside and play and wait for her to finish.

When we came home Mum would throw her feet up on the balcony rail, roll off her stockings and smoke her cigarettes in the sun. Maybe chat with the other women, but most of them were messed up, climbing those walls, trying to forget. It wasn't a good time for the women, losing their children.

Anyway, all the women folk were sitting up there this hot afternoon when down on the path arrived this white man, all suited up. Mum called down to him – I don't know why, she didn't know him. I remember she said, 'Hey there, mister, what you got there?'

A box was tucked under his arm. He looked up at us all and smiled. He come dashing up the stairwell and out onto our balcony. I think he would've been the only white person to ever step up there. He was smooth. 'Good afternoon to you, ladies, I am carrying in this box the best saucepans in the land.'

Mum drew back on her cigarette and stubbed it out in the tin. 'Give us a look then.'

The suit opened up the box and arranged the saucepans on the balcony, the sun making the steel shine and twinkle. They were magical. All the women whooped and whooed. The saucepans really were perfect. Five different size pans and a Dutch oven, for cakes. Strong, black, grooved handles on the sides and the lids, the real deal.

'How much?' Mum said, getting straight to the point.

The suit started up then on his big speech: Rena Ware, 18/10, only the best, and this and that, lifetime guarantee, all that sort of stuff.

The women started laughing. They knew what the punchline was going to be: nothing that they could afford, ever. Their laughter cascaded over the balcony rails as they followed each other back into the shade of their rooms.

'Steady on there, Alice, you got a little one to feed there too!' they said, seeing Mum entranced, watching his mouth move and the sun bouncing off the pans.

He told her the price, something ridiculous, and Mum didn't even flinch. She lit up another fag, puffed away. I think he was surprised, maybe relieved she didn't throw him out. He rounded up his speech, and Mum just sat there as he packed up the saucepans.

'You not gunna let me buy 'em then?' Mum said, blowing smoke over our heads.

'Would you like to, Miss?'

'Of course I bloody do. Wouldna sat here waiting for you to finish if I didn't!'

Mum told him then that she couldn't afford it, but she wanted them. So they made a deal. Samuel, the travelling salesman, would come by once a month, when money would arrive from the family, and take a payment each time.

Mum worked extra hours from then on, sometimes taking home the ironing, hoping to get a little more from the lady of the house. And she did, just enough. And Samuel would come round and chat with Mum and the other ladies and bring sweets for me. He and Mum would be chatting and drinking tea in the lounge until it got dark outside. They were friends after all that time.

Three years and seven months it took her. When Samuel came round on his last visit, with a box under his arm, just like the first time, Mum smiled big. He came into the flat and placed the box on the kitchen bench.

'Open it,' he said to Mum, and smiled down at me and winked.

Mum pressed her hands along the sides of her uniform then folded open the flaps and lifted out each saucepan, weighing it in her hands, squinting over at Samuel, puzzled. With each lid she took off, her tears gathered and fell.

'What is it, what is it?' I was saying as I pulled a chair up against the bench and could see then in one pan was a big leg of meat, under another lid potatoes and carrots, a shiny chopping knife, then a bunch of eggs, then bread. And in the Dutch oven, a wonky-looking steamed pudding.

Mum was crying too much to laugh at the cake.

'I haven't got a hand for baking yet. Hope you don't mind I tested it out.'

Mum just shook her head; she couldn't say a word and Samuel understood. He put on his smart hat, tilting the brim at Mum, and as he left the doorway, he said, 'Good day to you, Alice. Good day, young lady.'

And when Mum passed, she gave the pots to me.

When our mother finished her story she'd be crying too, tiny streams down her cheekbones. I knew she would hock everything we'd ever own, except the only thing that mattered, five size-ranged saucepans, with Dutch oven. Still in their hard case, only a few handles chipped.

I run my fingertips over fingerprints now, over years, generations. They haven't changed much; they still smell of friendship. I suppose that to my nanna, Samuel was much like a cloud buster. Letting in the sun, some hope, the rainbow had been their friendship. And I suppose that to Mum, Samuel was someone who she wanted to be around, like a blue sky. For Samuel, my mum and Nanna, I don't know, maybe the exchange *was* even, and maybe when those clouds burst open, he got to feel the rain. A cleansing rain, and maybe that was enough.

Waltzing Matilda

Herb Wharton

Herb Wharton was born in 1936 in Cunnamulla, Queensland. His published works include *Unbranded*, *Cattle Camp* and *Where Ya' Been, Mate?* In 1998 he received a residency at the Australia Council studio in Paris where he wrote *Yumba Days*, published in 1999. Herb was awarded the 2003 Centenary of Federation Medal for service to Australian society and literature, and in 2020 was made a Member of the Order of Australia (AM) for 'significant service to the literary arts, to poetry, and to the Indigenous community'.

Bunji and his old mate Knughy were droving horses in the outback. As the evening shadows lengthened they reached a billabong where the thirsty horses trotted down the sloping bank to drink heartily after their fifty-kilometre stage that day. Both Bunji and Knughy lived nomadic lives, wandering the stock routes droving sheep, cattle and horses, mainly for other people around the outback.

After the horses had watered, the two men looked around for a suitable camping place and unloaded their packhorse under a big, spreading old coolabah tree which would shelter them from the wintry night dew. While Knughy hobbled the horses close by, Bunji gathered firewood. Looking through their meagre rations, he realised they were out of meat – and there was very little else in the packs except for a bit of flour, some tea and sugar and a few spuds and onions.

'We got no *yudie* (meat)!' he called out.

'Might be we get 'em *thum-ba* (sheep) later on,' Knughy said. 'Plenty meat then.' He walked back to the camp, where the fire was now alight and the billy filled with water. Both men sat around the campfire waiting for a well-earned drink of tea.

At the moment, not two metres away, slowly lumbering down to the water like some prehistoric creature, they both saw this big old sand goanna. His long red tongue flickered as he walked along with the gait of a heavyweight sumo wrestler. Seemingly unafraid, he paid little attention to the two tired, hungry drovers. As it happened, the land this big old goanna strutted over was once their tribal kingdom.

Now this goanna might have been considered smart or brave, perhaps, walking in front of two hungry Murris like this. Or maybe he thought he was protected under some newfangled *withoo* (white) laws. In fact, his appearance was both foolish and fatal.

Both Bunji and Knughy jumped up, grabbed themselves sticks, and into the tuckerbag went goanna. As soon as the fire had produced enough coals and ashes, they scratched a long shallow hole in the ground, filled it with the coals and ashes, and cooked that big goanna.

'Proper bush yudie this one,' Bunji said later, savouring the tasty white flesh together with some johnnie-cake.

'A feast fit for a king,' Knughy agreed.

Bellies filled and pannikins brimful of tea, they sat around yarning, talking of the past, present and future. Bunji, who was about thirty, had been to school and was an inquiring sort of bloke. He'd worked in town and city and was an avid book reader, always in search of fresh knowledge.

Knughy, on the other hand, was old – how old, no one seemed to know. Some other old men even declared that Knughy was old when *they* were boys long ago. How old he really was is anybody's guess. His education came from mustering and droving and Murri camps: his learning from the land. He could read the land like a book. For him it told stories just like printed words and he still signed his name with a cross – yet he could decipher cattle, sheep and horse brands and over the years he had gained much knowledge of his tribal land and its laws, both past and present.

As the sun sank lower and the trees cast longer shadows, the birds flew in to drink at the billabong, screeching and cackling. Some hovered at its edge, others perched on protruding logs. Then a mob of bleating sheep came cavorting down the bank to drink there too, spreading right along the edge of the billabong and taking over from the birds.

'Bloody stupid animals, thum-bas,' said Knughy.

'Yes,' replied Bunji. 'Only things sillier are people who try to work them without a dog.' Then an idea came to him. 'Hey, let's get one of them!' he said. 'Him fill up tuckerbag good and proper.'

'No, no,' said Knughy, 'too close to the road here. Might be station owner come along – might be *Ghung-a-ble* (police) come along. Where you be then, hey?'

'Might be if Ghungie come I jump on horse and gallop away bush. Might be I jump into waterhole and swim away,' Bunji said.

'Might be you get caught ... might be you drown ... 'cause this is a funny waterhole, you know,' Knughy told him.

'Hey, what d'you know about this place?' Bunji asked.

And now he recalled that it was called Combo waterhole, and it was supposed to be here the Jolly Swagman had stolen a thum-ba from Dagworth Station as he camped ... maybe under this very coolabah tree. He had been surprised by the police, jumped into the waterhole and drowned. Bunji explained this piece of withoo history to Knughy in detail, and told him how it led Banjo Paterson to write the song 'Waltzing Matilda'.

'There's real, real history in this place, old man,' Bunji said.

'Might be this a good place, might be this a bad place,' the old man replied. His features were like dark, weathered leather. 'Might be this a real bad place ... might be *whonboo* (ghost) here too.'

'What do *you* know about this place, old man? Tell me,' urged Bunji.

By this time the sheep had gone bleating away, the sun had set, a few frogs croaked in the billabong and from the tree branches came the subdued *carkle carkle carkle* of the roosting birds.

'You know,' Bunji said, 'I've been reading and listening to a lot of different stories about that Jolly Swagman and don't know what to believe or think about him. What d'you reckon, old man?'

'Well, my boy,' said Knughy, knocking his bent-stemmed pipe against the coolabah tree before filling it with tobacco which he cut from a square, dark plug. 'Lotta history about here all right. Now you take that so-called Jolly Swagman – how d'you reckon a swaggie would feel jolly after tramping all day with his tuckerbag empty, belly pinching – might be his feet been aching too. Might be he had other problems, like he make 'em big *bhudie* (fire) in sacred place longa woolshed where they shear them thum-ba ...

'I can tell you that long time before all that happen, people still came walking here. This waterhole was proper sit-down place then, with plenty yudie, plenty fish, sugar-bag (honey) too. These people, they all belonga this land and they say – if you want 'em tucker you take 'em yudie. There weren't no branded or earmarked animals in them days. The laws said you could take 'em yudie if you was hungry. And it might be, like that swagman, after they sitting down a while, they move on to hunt another place.

'By and by other tribes come with horses, cattle, sheep and all the proper yudie become scarce. People don't belong to land no more, the land belong to people, and the animals too. This mob, they start walkabout looking for proper sit-down place, and if they come to place where others sit down first, those people say, "You fella gotta move on. We here first, this our sit-down place."

'Now I don't know about that swagman. Might be he come along hopeful and happy, looking for sit-down place, might be he feeling real jolly with his tuckerbag empty, belly pinching and feet aching. Then them thum-bas come down to water while he's sitting under this coolabah tree with his billy on the boil. Well, he grabs one, butchers it up and has a big feed. He real Jolly Swagman then, belly bulging, tuckerbag full. He sits there singing, no worries – and that's when them Ghungies come riding silently along. They seen that thum-ba's fresh skin, no meat in it, in the creekbed. "Hey, that's strange," they think. Might be someone been steal thum-ba belonging to big fella boss owns country, owns animals – might be his own Ghungies, too.

'But he don't own Jolly Swagman. The Ghungies hear this happy singing and ride up, yelling: "We've got you red-handed. Where's your dilly bag with the yudie in it belonging to *mar-thar* (boss)?" – "I'm the singing swagman. Ya can have the squatter's meat. Take my bloody swag as well! Prison bars won't shut me in! I'll escape across the water!" – Then he jumps into the billabong, swims like a man possessed – until, with the opposite bank and freedom in his sight, suddenly he turns and begins to wave his arms like a band conductor, starts singing out of tune – and sinks.' Knughy paused. 'One of them Ghungies, I bin told, remembered that swagman's song, and that's how the music came about.' He refilled his pipe, then went on: 'Others say the swagman was swearing at the Ghungies as he sank, screaming: "I'll come back to haunt youse, you hacks of landed gents!" And then he sank beneath the muddy brown water – pulled down with cramps, some say. But others say that other, more knowing eyes were watching from their hiding-place, and the Jolly Swagman was pulled down by the great water spirit, the *Munta-gutta*.'

As Knughy paused again to tamp down the tobacco in his pipe, from across the water came a screeching sound like a banshee, followed by loud splashing sounds like a flock of ducks landing. It was so loud it startled the horses feeding close by. Hobble chains clinked and horse bells donged as the animals gave restless jumps.

'What you reckon that is?' said Bunji nervously.

'Oh, maybe it's ducks landing – but then they usually sing out. And maybe that screaming sound is curlews.' Knughy shrugged. 'But to get back to the history of that swagman. Here's another version. Might be he came from that big sit-down place over that way' – he pointed with arm extended in a south-easterly direction. 'Well, over there they have been having this big bubblie and they bin fighting with the Ghungies. Afterwards this swagman goes walkabout, see, and might be he starts this bhudie (fire) in the mar-thar (boss cockie) sacred site, where them thum-bas are shorn. Then he comes along here, happy and singing, heading back to his proper sit-down place. But soon he begins to feel hungry and tired, so he camps here under this tree. He feels in his dilly bag – nothing there, no yudie, no *mhuntha* (bread); he got tea and sugar, billycan, swag, butcher knife. That's all. His belly's pinching. Soon some thum-bas come down thirsty – they want *gummu* (water). Well, that Jolly Swagman, he's real happy now. He grabs one of them thum-bas and soon he's singing again, no worries. The billycan's boiling, the dilly bag's full of yudie and his belly's bulging. He's singing so loudly he can't hear the horses coming ... the Ghungies ride up and find him. They don't know for sure if he stole that thum-ba or set that bhudie in the mar-thar sacred place, but they say, "We got ya now red-handed! Give yerself up, we're the law!"'

Once again old Knughy paused to refill his pipe. 'And that's when the Jolly singing Swagman made his fatal mistake,' he continued. 'He decided to go for a swim.'

'But didn't he make a mistake when he stole that sheep and burnt down the shearing shed?' Bunji interjected. 'He might have got away with both those things.'

'No, no,' Knughy replied. 'Young fellas like you should learn from this story.'

'What can I learn?' asked Bunji. 'Don't steal sheep, be careful where I light a fire, don't try to escape from lawful custody – is that all, old man?'

Knughy shook his head emphatically. 'The point is this: under no circumstances should you dive into deep water with a full belly. That's what killed that Jolly Swagman, my boy – going for a swim on a full belly.'

Bunji closed his eyes and sat silently for a moment, pondering this new-found information. Then, his eyes still closed, he asked: 'But what about them sounds, what about the Munta-gutta, what about the whonboo (ghost), what about …' He rambled on, but soon discovered he was talking to himself. For Knughy had silently slipped away, rolled out his swag, and was soon snoring his head off.

Bunji got up, looked around warily, then pulled his own swag closer to the old man. His mind was in turmoil. What could he believe? What was fact, what was fiction? What was reality, what was myth? Was history true or false? Suddenly he recollected an image of the past, and recalled the words of wisdom from his mother. She had always insisted: 'My boy, never but *never* swim on a full stomach.'

Could that really have been the cause of the death of the Jolly Swagman, he wondered.

Shadows on the Wall

Archie Weller

Archie Weller was born in 1957. His first novel, *The Day of the Dog*, was shortlisted for the Vogel Award and won the fiction award in the literature section of the Western Australian Week Literary Awards. Archie has also published *Land of the Golden Clouds* and *Going Home*, an acclaimed collection of short stories, plays and poems.

It started over a cigarette. Such simple things are a big issue when strangers are crammed into small spaces under a great deal of duress.

'Gnummerai-wa, coodah,' he croaked after being tossed into the cell unceremoniously. The shaven-headed white man ignored him as he had ignored the other youth all evening. The other youth who now made the hand sign for 'nothing'.

He did have cigarettes but he wasn't sharing them with this pugnacious stranger who had been aggressive the moment the constable in charge of this town manhandled him through the door of the police station. In fact the violence that radiated from him like writhing serpents of smoke frightened the placid youth and besides he needed the smokes for tomorrow when he was released and his hangover hit him. So he pretended he had nothing and let the thin Nyoongah pace the small area of the cell in agitation and boiling anger not cured by a calming cigarette. They didn't even observe the usual Nyoongah courtesy of trading names, working out who someone was and where they fit in.

In the dark hours of early morning he went to have a quiet smoke then turned, sensing the hot gaze on him.

'Wanker! Shove ya poxy smokes up ya tight kwon. Anyone ud think they was made of solid gold, ya stingy bastard.' But this was the tiny bit of power he wielded – who can and cannot have a smoke. He smiled at the angry stranger who grumbled then rolled over to go to sleep. But the stranger didn't let it go forgotten. The person had broken a code of the street – to share whatever anyone had as no-one had much of anything.

All the next day there had been smouldering silent resentment and the odd barbed comment, the white man observing the hidden violence seething in the youth's chest, being cynically amused. He looked on the one youth as a little bantam rooster strutting in a filthy barnyard thinking himself king of the world and the other youth as a pathetic drunk. Both were abos, people least deserving of this man's sympathy – if he had any to give. But it had amused him wondering what interesting developments might occur in this tiny space between the two and was disappointed when there was only stifling resentment and deliberate disregard. A good barney would have livened up the day spent in this boring no-name town.

As to the two Nyoongahs they ignored the white man, the one because he hated all white people and the other because he was shy of strangers coming into his little world – especially a stranger as big and dangerous as this man appeared to be.

Pale sunshine crept through the rusty wire mesh on the window as the last light of day sent their shadows dancing blackly on the wall as they paced restlessly up and down. The older youth was darker than the younger one, more thin than slim, with pigeon chest, skinny arms covered in scrawled ink tattoos explaining his love life with various female names, his thoughts – on his left upper arm some sort of flower and 'Mum foreva' written by a less than skilful hand – or attempts of art like the spider's web splaying outwards from his elbow down his right arm.

His nickname was 'Spider' and he carried it with pride. Some, like the white man observing these two, would have said no such emotion resided in his bony body, with his shifty downcast eyes and shuffling feet. They didn't know his mind that burned like a fiery furnace and the knowledge he carried with him everywhere – the name his father had left him with and who his father was.

His father had murdered two innocent lovers down on an isolated beach one balmy summer's night. He had come across them while they hugged in passionate embrace and after tying them up had robbed them then raped the woman then murdered them both. He got life for murder and had even been on death row before it was abolished and committed suicide when he could no longer take a life forever behind bars. Yes, Spider found out all about Benjy Cockles when he was just twelve years old from a woman in the park who said she was Benjy's cousin. He kept that name like a warrior would keep a medal for it made him who he was.

Bleak eyes look out of a sullen face while he thinks up some comment to annoy the other Nyoongah in the cell – Mr Tight-arse who couldn't even share a single poxy smoke. He was angry with himself for becoming trapped like a dingo in this useless dusty town; caught like a novice as this dirty smelly youth must be instead of the professional he was. He had given a false name but it should not take the constable long to figure out who he really was with his tattoos on show. So he paced angrily like a caged lion, wishing himself far away from this place.

The other youth, a local lad, had been in here countless times. He wasn't bad, just stupid, his peers and elders said. He enjoyed a drop, others said kindly. The truth – at twenty-three he had given up on life, a hopeless drunk, never doing anything violent or vicious, letting the warm red port or cool amber beer soak through his body. He would sing songs, crack jokes and be the clown. Except sometimes he sang too loudly or his jokes weren't funny to some people or his clownish antics only annoyed and did not amuse his audience. Then he ended up here.

He paced because he was hanging out for a drink. Usually he was let out to tend the garden the constable's wife had going, getting up a bit of a sweat, finding his own way back to the cell left open for him. Where would he run to if he did decide to escape? The next town was over a hundred kilometres away. He was good old Gary, a harmless drunk who had started drinking young and would die young of a ruined liver and no one would miss him at all.

But overnight two strangers came into the little town's world. Spider, slipping like a ghost through the darkening streets, had just his shadow for company as always. Thinking himself safe in this outback hamlet he had done what came natural to him: break into a residence for food, drink, perhaps a blanket or coat to keep warm as he went his transitional way; but was caught climbing out the window like a first-timer.

Meanwhile the large white man was being transferred to Perth when the prison van broke down – these private companies who ran prisons now were noticeably incompetent – forcing them to stay over in Gary's town and Gary's home. It was what the constable had chuckled at as he let the beefy shaven-headed man with his cold blue eyes into the cell.

'You've got a guest tonight, Gaz, so be the good host and show him the ropes,' he grinned and Gary sensed with a growing despondency he would be staying inside his whole term this time. He tried a smile but the big white man turned his back ignoring him scornfully to stare out the barbed and meshed window. No escape there either, he thought. He hunched down angrily in the corner.

I could have made it, he thinks. *Be in Thailand, Vietnam or any Asian country, sipping ice-cold drinks with a couple of young Asian beauties sitting naked beside me.*

But that jealous bitch in Darwin ...

'I'll just get a pizza, Donny, darling. I'll bet they don't have pizzas in Indonesia,' she had said, knowing full well she hadn't been invited.

He should have realised – the smartest bank robber in the country who had done over fifteen banks in three years. Not just small amounts either but thousands, organising the jobs carefully; doing it by himself or with his brother – with clever disguises and meticulous planning. They had had enough stashed away for a rich and peaceful life among the jungles of a poor but safe foreign land. They would be kings ...

He smells the salt air of the port. Tonight his brother has paid a cargo ship captain to sail them over to Jakarta. He can taste freedom on his lips that curl upwards in a cynical superior smile. He can hear muted laughter of golden-skinned girls with sloe-black eyes and exquisitely formed lips and hips. He can see the mansion he and his brother will buy with walls so white they hurt the eyes, a swimming pool so blue it hurts the senses, his own personal bar like he has seen on movies. He ... and his brother ... will be richer than any movie star.

Quick furtive shadowy figures against the window. Before he can grab the gun beside him or make his escape, the door bursts in and shouting screaming men pour in to hurl him from out of the bed and out of his dreams.

His father was right, he thinks. *'Never, ever trust a sheila,' his father had said the last time he saw him. 'I trusted your mother and she ran out on us, remember?' And how could he forget, for it was then his father turned to crime to support a couple of growing lads. But he was never a good thief and now he lay, emaciated from cancer that gnawed away at him, lying in the narrow uncomfortable prison bed covered in thin grey blankets and none-too-clean sheets.*

If the truth was to be told his father had run out on them, being the unsuccessful crook he was, always getting caught for pissy little jobs that never amounted to much. They could have been a happy family if he had settled down instead of spending his life in and out of jail. The oldest son had vowed never to be like that. That is the gift his father left him. Because now he was a well-known, much-feared man – Donny Betts, wanted Australia-wide – but in the end he was his father's son after all, getting caught by the honeyed snares of a woman – blonde-haired, blue-eyed, brown-skinned, good in bed, no brains ... he had thought.

At least his brother will get away. Loyal to his family, no amount of threats or coercion forced him to give Jimbo up but he knows he can't see him for a long time and this upsets him for they had been very close: Donny and Jimbo – more best mates than brothers and what did they say: you can choose your mates but not your family. He knows that if he is ever released he can live out his old age in the tatters of the dreams he held like fine silk once not so long ago.

But did he only imagine the looks passing between his brother and that bitch as he was dragged out of the motel room?

Now he was stuck in this cell with life's losers snarling at each other. On principle he had nothing to do with abos – the one time he had been inside showed him they were mostly petty crims in for moronic incidents: shitty little break and enters, stealing cars and generally crashing them, home invasions, rape. They were annoying little black flies buzzing around his head. They were cowards, drugged-out fuck-ups and dogs the lot of them.

All his conceptions appeared true as he watched the bleary dopey eyes of the one and the agitated movements of the other – a drunkard and a petty thief, that about summed the whole race up, he thought. He would be amused if his own predicament were not so serious. He had thought there might be a slim chance of breaking out of this one-horse town but listening to the dopey one's comments it seemed that breaking out he would have nowhere to go.

'What do we do for a cup of tea around 'ere, Mr Bojangles?' Spider rasped.

'Give the constable a loverly big kiss, broh. 'e'll soon butter up ya arse.'

27

Silence fell once more upon the dingy room. Spider's quick mind worked overtime planning to escape this dilemma. Perhaps the police were as stupid as his cellmate. Perhaps they wouldn't recognise him. He had heard of a prisoner arrested for a minor misdemeanour then let loose the next day, when he was wanted in three states.

'When's the Judge comin'? You reckon I'll just get a fine or what?'

'What ya do, broh?'

'Nicked a blanket to keep warm and some food.'

'Oh, regular Al Capone, unna! Judge give ya years for that, bud. Fuckin' years!' Gary smiled, pleased at the consternation his words put on his tormenter's face.

He sang softly to himself, an Elvis Presley song he loved.

'Don't be cru-u-el to a heart that's true.'

His mother had given 'Elvis' as his second name – Gary Elvis Mindari – often telling him he would be as good a singer one day. So he grew up with Elvis Presley songs and Elvis Presley movies. He styled himself on the great man when he was younger and had dreamed of becoming as famous a singer one day.

A standing joke between Gary and the constable every time he was released was that he would fling back an imaginary cape and utter in perfect imitation:

'Thank you very much ... Elvis has now just left the building.' It never failed to get a chuckle.

Yes, 'Than'-you-very-much,' he would mutter Elvis-like from the side of his mouth as he stepped out into the morning. But he would not hear the birds sing or see the sun rise. He only thought of when the pub would be opening. Sometimes he would mutter to himself, also in Elvis-mode, 'This one's for you, Mama,' and let the memories flow in.

He laughed now, thinking about the drink he would buy with his last twenty bucks and set his mind to thinking who he could bludge off until next dole day.

'What have you got to laugh about ya dopey prick?' Spider growled, echoing the big white man's thoughts exactly. 'Ya better not be laughin' at me!'

'Why not, bud! You as funny as a barrel of monkeys. And not one key opens the door,' Gary chuckled.

Spider snorted angrily. He could smell the alcohol from right across the room. He never had anything to do with alcohol, keeping away from solvents and speed and other heavy drugs as well, that had ruined so many of his peers. A sharp clear mind was what was needed if life had dealt you a crappy hand.

The shadow jerks on the bright cartoon pattern of the walls of the room. His very own, he had been told. He is special, he has been told, and so it seems for he has his own room, a Game Boy, PlayStation, his own stereo and a chest full of the latest toys. He even has a few friends at school so on weekends sometimes they come to play and there are barbecues, cruises on the launch his father is so proud of.

Not his real father of course. Not his real mother either, but the only family he has ever known. Smiling red faces, merry blue eyes, lots of joking around amidst the discipline. Pats on the curly head, friendly taps on the bottom, a kiss goodnight.

Here he comes now. Shadows jerk against the bright patterns of

Bart Simpson, Homer, Marge and the others, Donald Duck, Bugs Bunny and all the crew. But they can't help him just as his friends at school can't help him. Trapped in a soft silken cocoon like the spider's victim. Here comes the spider now with soft words and empty eyes oozing smiles and a hand, soft and white as pus creeping under the sheet to crawl upon his skin.

They call paedophiles rock spiders in prison slang. But he was called Spider because he had absolutely no mercy at all – just like his real father.

He had kept away from home as often as he could when he became aware the games his foster-father played were not right. He blamed himself and was headed down the path of shame and confusion and degradation, leading to alcohol and drug abuse. All the presents in the world and the love of a woman who, he sensed, would take the side of her husband were not worth it.

So he left, choosing his own path in life. He found pleasure sneaking into other people's bedrooms and taking their Game Boys, stereos, DVD recorders or whatever else he wanted. He owned any house in the city – a powerful person and a much better high than any drugs or drink could give him. If he was arrested he was usually out within the month or two. But when he was thirteen he stabbed his first victim, another street kid, in a fight over a pair of Nikes. By the time he was twenty he had spent six months in the big boys' prison and gained a reputation, just as his father had, of being a hard violent man best left alone.

★

He was up in this forgotten part of the world because his anger had finally boiled over when, lounging on the street, he saw his former foster-father, near the park, proposition a boy Spider vaguely knew, who was high on solvent abuse and didn't know what he was doing.

Spider darted forwards, enjoying the surprise on his victim's face, then the complacent smile of recognition, then the look of horror and disbelief as the long wicked knife slid home, through silk suit, through puffy white skin into where his heart should have been.

But Spider knew the boy he had saved would have no loyalty towards him. He was no kin whatsoever. He would dob him in and, like his father, he would be jailed forever.

He had been heading out to places unknown, perhaps to find the mother he could not even remember, just the faint recollection of a warm brown breast feeding him warm milk and a fuzzy memory of a gentle smiling face. It was always his dream to find his mother one day. The rose and the words had been his first tattoo, put on his skinny arm by an older street kid when he was only ten. A rose to remind him of his mum's name from a half-remembered story some old woman had told him.

'You ain't nothin' but a hound dog, howlin' all the time,' Gary sang, looking directly at him.

'For Crise sakes, ya know any modern songs? What about Notorious BIG?'

'What about 'im? Dead, ain't 'e!?'

'So's bloody Elvis.'

'Not to me he isn't, broh. Me and Mum used to love Elvis.'

His father also has the second name of Elvis, his mother tells him when he is only three: 'The Black Elvis we yorgas used to call 'im,' she says. 'Deadly dancer ya dad and sing like a bird he could.'

The world is still a fine place for a chubby happy three-year-old. A happy life in a peaceful town. They are the only Nyoongahs left when there had once been many living on the old Reserve outside of town: Mindaris, Funnells, Whites, Feathers, Pigeons ...

As he gets older he shows an interest in football, becoming almost a star on the team that never won a premiership. He dreams of becoming a fabulously wealthy singer and the highlight of his life was winning the talent show the town put on as a fundraiser once. He dreams of moving away to far-off Perth and doing a music course or becoming an electrician or mechanic. He spends so much time dreaming he never gets anywhere.

His mother enjoys a drink – until the memories hit her like a brick. She drinks to drown out past sadness and memories. One of them is when the Welfare women came and took away her first-born, she once tells a surprised Gary, interested slightly to learn he has a brother somewhere. Taken because she and her man were deemed unfit parents. So his mother drinks from sorrow and this he can understand; knows something of her pain. He tried to be like the son she had lost to take away that pain but he could not even succeed at that. It bothered him too. Once, before he was born, there had been another Elvis, yet nothing remained of him ... not a photo ... nothing but his mother's anguish – but he is in the building now!

When she dies she is only fifty-one and he is just eighteen. His world dies too. Realising life is passing him by with nothing much to show for it he sinks even deeper into apathy. His fantasies are sometimes peopled by an image of a brother come to rescue him from this life, a rich and famous brother ... a famous sportsman maybe or a wealthy member of society who will help him in his ambitions. But he soon gives up on his tenuous hold on dreams for the reality is his brother is gone. One by one the mocking dreams float unattainable into the sky until all he has left is his jokes and Friday Night Karaoke when, for a while, he is a star again. That'll do him, he thinks, downing another cask of Fruity Lexia. He has forgotten the brother he never knew. He also never knew his wandering father. He loved his mother, who was taken so young, and he loves this little town ... and Elvis Presley songs ... and his wine.

He sees the shadow of his mother everywhere. It is why he will never leave this town.

'Come on, ya fuckwit. I ast ya polite-like now I'm tellin' ya! What about this Judge! Is 'e likely to slap me 'and then send me on me way? I never stole much anyrate, just some meat outa the fridge and a poxy blanket off the line.'

'Yeah, I seen that blanket. Ya couldn't pinch a better one than that old grey thing? What! Are you the Grey Ghost?' Gary grinned.

'The Judge! Is 'e a bastard or what?!'

'Probably give ya fifty years for stealin' that blanket. On the chain gang,' Gary said deadpan then laughed. 'Naaah, just let ya out on community work, most prob'ly. Sometimes he offers a kid 'e'll buy them a bike if they be'ave.' He looked the skinny, tattooed stranger up and down and grinned again. 'But you look a bit too old for bikes, unna!'

★

The outer door to the office opened. The constable walked in with a triumphant look on his face. Behind him are the two drivers of the prison van.

'Elvis Cockle?' he said, looking directly at Spider, then smiled wider when he saw the furtive reaction. 'Yes ... the rose tattoo. Well, chum, you're not seeing your mum any time soon. The bloke you stabbed died last night. Some people want to talk to you in Perth right now!'

Just for a second the two youths' shadows merged as one on the grimy wall before the door clanged open and the two warders from the repaired van stomped business-like into the cell to hustle him and the white man outside.

They had to get these two dangerous criminals quickly into the van. Too often this particular company had messed up with people dying in vans, one famous escape involving seven prisoners ... They would not make a mistake like that!

First bewilderment and then, understanding, a little light lit up in his dull eyes.

'Elvis Cockle,' Gary said in a whisper. 'Hey, you're my brother,' he called after the hastily retreating men. 'We got the same mother,' he sang out a pathetic song to the sound of the clashing crashing closing door.

But he did not know if he had been heard.

He sank down in the corner, huddling against the wall – just his shadow and himself – like it had always been.

'Broh! Ngooni!' he whispered. 'You and me got the same mum, Rosalind Mindari. I'm your brother, Gary Elvis Mindari, man!'

Outside, Spider is shoved unceremoniously into the hard iron insides of the van with the wadjela. The van takes off with a roar, jolting them as the heavy vehicle lumbers towards distant captivity. His shadow bounces on the hard iron wall. He often said his shadow was his only friend.

All his life he had searched for his mother. He does not care about the man he murdered. He does not care about the bitter man he shares this space with. He does not care about his father whose tales of aggression have kept him going all these years. By some twist of fate he had paced the cell most of the night and all that day just a handshake away from his blood relative, his only close relative ... his brother. And he had only thought how useless the drunkard had been.

... 'Don't be cru-u-el to a heart that's true ...'

He turned his head to the heavily barred window. For the first time in years, hot tears trickle down his cheek.

'Here, broh,' said the white man recently separated from his own brother for many years – even a brother that had probably betrayed him in the end – 'have a smoke,' he says gently.

For sometimes it is the smallest thing that can bring comfort. They both knew that.

Glossary

coodah	brother
Gnummerai-wa	Do you have a cigarette?
kwon	arse
ngooni	brother
Nyoongah	Aboriginal people of south-west Australia
Unna isn't it?	Is that true?
wadjela	white person

The Release

Samuel Wagan Watson

Samuel Wagan Watson is an award-winning Indigenous poet of Munanjali, Birri Gubba, German and Irish descent. Samuel's fourth poetry collection, *Smoke Encrypted Whispers*, won the 2005 NSW Premier's Literary Award for Book of the Year and the Kenneth Slessor Prize. He has been a writer in residence at a number of institutions and has toured New Zealand, Germany and Norway to promote his work.

D anny and Bull ... Bull and Danny.
Some final splinters of sunlight jagged the hilltops on
the western rises before them. Danny drove. The petrol gauge
read half a tank. He and his cousin Bull would never have been
caught dead in these remnants of day when they were kids.
Elders had warned of red-eyes appearing on the edge of the
unsealed road; meandering spectres making their journeys to
haunt, claiming unpaid debts from the living. Bull rode in the
passenger seat of the car. Danny had promised Bull's mother
that they'd be home by dusk.

The sedan was reasonably new and slick; slick for this region
anyway, carrying two dark passengers up the winding roads
of the big valley that coursed west from River City. Danny
couldn't help feeling like a black wraith moving through the
numerous ghost towns on the back roads towards Murgon. As
the pair climbed into the ranges the sentinels of Bunya Pine
became more prominent; Black Cockatoo country.

'You wanna stop 'ere in Fernvale ... Get a sixpack for the
drive?'

Danny had heard that wayward anticipation in his cousin's
voice. 'Nah ... I promised your mother, Bull ...'

The vehicle had already drawn stares from night owls. There were no 'Welcome' mats in these tiny communities. A blackfulla from the city knew this in his blood. The people out here had a gentle way as they moved. Arthritic hate. A bent neck that eased an arch at strangers.

A flatland of shadows unfolded out of gumtrees and thicket. Danny smelt the familiarity of lavender farms. 'We're almost there, Bull.'

His cousin had been quite subdued along the trip. Even when they passed Wacol and the prison where Bull had been a 'guest', the energy in the car was flat. There was nothing Danny wanted to say anyway. Some of the bricks had fallen down from the childhood bond the men had built together. Danny chose the city. Bull earned a cracked pelvis on the rodeo circuit. Bull found it hard to even ride a lawnmower after that. Then the broken cowboy consumed painkillers to chase the hurt. Alcohol ... Heroin ... Chapters in custodial detention.

Danny finally eased the car into Murgon. The suspension clapped over the dormant train crossing. White folk kept to their pub on the left. The black folk knew their place across the way. A solitary statue of an Anzac held residence in the main-street division. Danny looked over his shoulder briefly thinking he might see the lights of Cherbourg Mission behind the township, but there wasn't even a firefly's chance. Out of mind, out of sight. Some traffic loomed. A couple of dark faces checked up from their drinks. This was a bubble that would take decades to deflate and decolonise.

'You wanna stop in for one?' asked Bull.

Danny calmly exhaled, ignoring his cousin's voice. He

glanced into the side streets. The constabulary weren't even lurking. A blackfulla driving a new, registered and reliable vehicle could warrant a mandatory search among this 'small-town' silt.

'Not far now,' whispered Danny.

Solar flares were burring in the crests ahead of them. There was no oncoming traffic. Danny wondered for a moment whether or not he should tweak the headlights to high beam and then decided against it. Black wings of a crow sprang before the car. Roadkill tarnished bitumen. A crossroad loomed. Danny recognised the silhouette of a broken sulky in a barren paddock. Fingers of rustling cane. Unkept fences. He aimed the car in a gentle manner onto a winding road that soon lost the smooth surface into wafting dust clouds.

'Remember when Stewie swore he saw a devil-dog on this track one night?' Then the hairs sprang on the back of Danny's neck. He regretted the memory instantly. The lore in isolation of this place had earned his respect; some fear, but mostly a healthy respect. Bull's father, who was dead now for thirty years, had tried to make his peace with the spectral matters here too. But there was little point in keeping shades of the afterlife away. 'Old Bull' often recounted the tales of settlers who went missing in these hills and how the winter months harboured their cries on the chilling tongue of wind.

Danny navigated in fragmented memory and weariness. This was a place where the mind's eye tricked you. A small patch of land sat ahead dropping into a gully. Failing daylight, but nonetheless, Danny had brought his cousin to a place that was a birthright. Wads of blade grass were almost covering the shoulders of the road now and a track veered off into nothing.

The headlights of the car were literally consumed in the wilds of undergrowth. And this was good. Safety in cover. A faceless bank manager had dispossessed the family any rights on the property for a generation. Danny and Bull had aspirations of working these ridges as kids; more so Bull than Danny but reality and economic rationalism hijacked those dreams. Danny would soon be forty-eight years old. And degenerative natures had made their way into Bull's body for some time now too.

Danny thought about his fading passenger, the pile of belongings in the car that were his only worldly possessions. Methadone. Demons. AHHH, BULL, WHAT DID THEY DO TO YOU IN PRISON??? Once upon a time their elders called the cheeky pair 'Amigos'.

Suddenly the wheels of the vehicle ran over metal. It must have been the forgotten cattle grid that was too choked by weeds to be seen and it brought them both out of their stupors.

'We're here, mate!' said Danny.

'I know,' chirped Bull.

Danny allowed gravity to do the rest and the vehicle rolled into a rough meadow next to the heap of a dilapidated dwelling. A sturdy hardwood frame of the four walls had collapsed in, bringing down a hood of corrugated iron. Small saplings were reclaiming floor. The sun was poor but enough to pose light on the dim mushroom cloud of a mango tree on the other side of the wreckage.

Bull's mother was too frail to even meet them up here. As Danny cranked the door open a maze of shrub and grass met him in contention. He realised he couldn't have even unfolded her wheelchair from the sedan to welcome her son home.

'Come on then.'

Strand and leaf fought against Danny as he waded out from the car. He felt the cool air suppress his frame. Green needles pricked. Footing was difficult at first. Blood began to circulate through his legs. The leather boots and heavy denim jeans he wore gave him enough confidence to blindly track through the tangles. He stomped metres and then turned back to the car.

Danny reached in and cut the ignition, flicking the headlights off. There was a calm and comfortable dimness that surrounded them. Bugs chirped. The sky almost mirrored the land in mats of luxuriant cloud morphing and jumbled as the earliest evening stars made an appearance. The moon was too low yet to really show any influence. In the pitch of this setting Danny felt his cousin ease too.

'I did promise your Mum, my Brother ... Sorry we couldn't stop.'

Danny and Bull were both of Wakka Wakka blood and had returned to the tribal country of their Wakka Wakka forebears. Bull's mother had seen the burial of too many Wakka Wakka kindred laid to rest in the Mission cemetery of scarred-red earth studded in white identical wooden crosses. The days of mourning and misery, misery and mourning, wave upon wave of Sorry business, no justice and no reckoning for the innocent and the wretched.

Danny stretched back into the car for a beige paper bag stamped 'PERSONAL PROPERTY' with the aid of a few remaining lights that flickered in the dashboard and the only light for miles around. He struggled to pull a flat container carefully away from the coupled garments and paperwork that some prison official had impersonally packaged.

'You alright there, Bull?' he gently whispered.

Firmly holding the container he stepped back into the grass and made trail upon the sodden growth. He moved about, the moisture of dusk gathering on the thickets until a clearing that gave access down into the folds of the land. Much motionless shadow and gullies beyond.

Danny paused and listened to his lush surroundings.

'Here were go, cobber,' he said. His throat dumped a solemn gulp. He puffed out his chest and called out to Bull: 'Ere, mate. You're home now!'

Danny carefully snapped the lid on the container and assumed an odour would follow; a smell that may possibly illustrate some of the prison stench; damp cold concrete and White Ox tobacco. Angst. The essence of what had become of his cousin, the ingredients of a man's life and pain. He let the ash sift before him into the night.

'There ya go, bud.'

Subtle breezes picked up the fine white powder and a rush of motion parted the grasses downhill and away. Little paper-winged moths flocked out of the growth and danced in the flow of Bull's departure. Danny saw fleeting seed lift from thickets, in unison with the clicks of tiny grasshoppers excitedly jumping into the dusk. Somewhere in the lower ridges a menagerie of bird noise erupted and a flowering bud of moonlight broke through cloud above the distant peaks of tree line. Bull's spiritual presence made small tumbling spirals that retreated into the shrub; finally at rest in playful communion with the country in the remains of the day. A pledge fulfilled.

'There ya go, Bull … There ya go … You're free.'

Danny and Bull … Bull and Danny … Amigos.

Each City

Ellen van Neerven

Ellen van Neerven is an award-winning writer of Mununjali Yugambeh (South East Queensland) and Dutch heritage. Ellen's first book, *Heat and Light*, was the recipient of the David Unaipon Award, the Dobbie Literary Award and the NSW Premier's Literary Awards Indigenous Writers Prize. They have written two poetry collections: *Comfort Food*, which was shortlisted for the NSW Premier's Literary Awards Kenneth Slessor Prize; and *Throat*, which was shortlisted for the Queensland Literary Awards and the Victorian Premier's Literary Awards.

1.

It isn't what we want to do but I need clean socks. And towels. We have run out of clean towels. Talvan sits on the washing machine as I count how many coins I have left. Enough to wash but not to dry.

The smell of laundry powder and a changing season. Talvan's boots tapping my shin. I run my fingers over the toe and smile in a way she knows. She stretches her foot out and asks me if I can dash into the store next door and pick her up some chocolate.

That Queensland sun prodding and calling from the window.

Talvan didn't have much to do at work today. She's started an identified position as a junior architect of the Indigenous Cities Unit, and the process has been stalled. Yep, if you hadn't heard, and you're only watching the mainstream news, they are not being built. Talvan was part of the team that designed the first two. It was a great idea: reduce the strain on Kadi-Naarm-Meanjin (Syd-Mel-Bris) by trying to get people living elsewhere, but everyone's going to be sorry in a little while.

The two cities, you know the one that's just north of Wagga, on Wiradjuri Country, which they are calling Wiradjuri City, and the other city, the one that removed my mother and the community, Mununjali City, 100 kilometres south of Meanjin. You remember the propaganda: *Get people living west! Away from the coastal clusters! Open space, community centres, all connected via fast speed rail! Create new jobs and housing! Be the fresh start you've dreamed of!* Yeah, Jimbelung. You stepped right into our dream.

We are laughing. She's scooping grey Bonds undies out of the machine and putting them into my sports bag, flirting with her lips, and I'm thinking about so much while we're walking home: kissing, and watermelon, and the beach. Some lyrics are maybe coming too, yes, the air feels poignant with meaning, and memory.

We pass the motorcycle shop where a guy's washing his bike; we walk around and smile at a mother and her two kids, still in their school uniform. The bins are still out, outside our place. That's not what troubles me. The gate's been left open. I drop the bag of wet clothes immediately.

'I think I left the back door open a bit, the sliding door …' Talvan is saying. 'What the f—'

'Careful, Talvan, stay with me …'

But I'm already running. I run inside and see that they or it or whatever it is has come, and they have seen everything.

My laptop is gone from the dining-room table. My box of notebooks from my study. Somehow I know exactly what they've taken.

'I burned some toast this morning …' Talvan touches my shoulder.

'Talvan, I'm going to check my studio.'

'No, not just yet.' She suddenly gets very frightened and holds me back.

'I'm going.'

'Okay, I'm coming with you.'

I slide the back door further ajar.

'It was open, I'm so sorry!'

'It wasn't your fault. They would have come in anyway. They knew what they were looking for.'

'We were only gone an hour at the most.'

'I know.' I reach for her hand as we walk across to the shed I've claimed as my creative space. A place I could make sound away from the main house as not to annoy Talvan and our ex-housemate, Holly, when she was living here.

Inside, all the recording equipment, the speakers, the mic, the Weaver system – are gone. Just a lonely sheet rack and a chair and rolls of paper left.

'We need to go,' Talvan says.

'I know,' I say, trying to move my head away from the devastating sight. 'I don't think we can go to your mum's. I'll ask Aunty Lou.'

'Why?'

'They might know ...' I take my phone out of my pocket, flick the screen.

'What are you doing?'

'Trying to change my password. And then I'm going to call Aunty Lou. From a payphone.'

My fingers hover over the tracks I've had finished this week. Sitting there in the cloud, as wavs and mp3s. I don't delete them. I do delete my contacts though, after copying them down on paper. Mum. Aunty Lou.

I try to talk to Talvan about what we should do next but she's saying she can't understand me and I realise I'm speaking lingo from out my way. Always talking Yugambeh when I'm proper stressed. I don't think I've ever been this stressed before. I wasn't helping my Noongar one out at all so I'd better speak 'English'.

'Pack a bag with some clothes. Some food. Get out a bag for me too, please. We'll head out and I'll call Aunty Lou and see where we should go, what we should do.'

Talvan nods. 'Do you want me to pack for you too?'

'Why?'

'I know how you find it tricky to pick things for a trip.'

'It doesn't matter.' I manage a smile. She knows how hard it would be to leave some of my sneakers and blackfella hoodies behind, if that's what we are doing, leaving things behind. 'Thanks.'

She runs upstairs and comes down exactly five minutes later with two backpacks.

'They've taken the chargers.'

'Put your phone on low light, you'll save battery.'

Our suburb feels rowdy when we leave. I have become scared of my neighbours. My street doesn't feel safe. Stepping over the bag of wet clothes as we leave, the bag that we've forgotten, the clothes we can't keep.

Aunty Lou's voice is immediate. I don't think the phone even rang.

'Who's this?'

'It's your niece.'

'Hello, love. You calling me from a payphone, what's the deal?'

I cover the phone with my hand and talk in hushed tones

even though there's nobody about.

'Bub, I told you what to do if this happened. You remember?'

'They are really following me, hey? Why me? I have a few songs up, nothing flash.'

I can hear Aunty Lou take a big sip of Earl Grey tea before she begins talking me up. 'Your work is powerful, young niece, and it's getting lots of attention. You got a strong, unfiltered voice exposing the realities of our people under this current government. It's not going unnoticed. And you know they are tightening the laws. Your hip ... hip-hop and just what you say could soon be enough for a prison sentence.'

'Hip-hop, yeah, Aunty.'

'Legally you should be protected. But you know they've got full and unrestricted access. They are tapping your phone, they know everything. They are going to make your life uncomfortable in any way they can.'

'Wait, so I'm on the list now? ASIO? I feel I'm like what you fellas had in the seventies. The stories you tell me about.'

'When they zoom in their evil eye, it stays there for a while.'

I look over at Talvan, standing back, and she smiles, but only out of habit.

'Stay offline. And think about getting away, another country, somewhere off the radar, until this blows over. Until it's safe. You shouldn't have any troubles getting out of the country. They don't have any power to stop you.'

'But they can stop me coming back in, right?'

'Yes, that's right, niece.'

'Okay, Aunty, I gotta go. We're gonna go bush for a while.'

'Yes, good. Stay offline.'

★

Talvan kisses me quickly, still managing to drive the shitty car her friend let us borrow.

'Babe, you can slow down for a sec, it's okay.'

'Yeah?'

Her eyes are still focused on the road ahead, the Klump Road exit shining up ahead.

'Yeah, babe, let's stop here and take a moment. Have a snack.'

She exits onto Klump Road and takes us round the back way of the school I went to for a few semesters when we lived on this side of town. She stops in the car park.

'You did Year Five here, right?' she says, gesturing to the lights of the hall.

'How did you remember that?'

'Because it was the start of Year Six when you and your mum and nanna moved next door to our place. I still remember the day. It was kind of the best day of my life.'

I break off a bit of the KitKat I bought her a few hours ago at the shop next to the laundromat. I offer it to her and she meets her mouth to mine. Everything is so overwhelming that my only thoughts are to comfort her and as we kiss she keeps her eyes open, staring into mine, the chocolate growing warmer in my palm. She wriggles her hips closer and we kiss deeper. Not until my hands are rolling up her skirt and I reclaim the terror that's been building up in me does she close her eyes, and after a few loose breaths, I close mine too. I rub the melted chocolate on her thighs. Move down to gently lick it off.

★

Approaching from the north, Mununjali City is abandoned construction and a whole lot of circles. Trucks and freight trains for miles.

Promises are dug out into the dirt, the dark soil of my ancestors. It's quiet. No trees, no birds. We drive for ages through this endless abandoned project.

'I'm sorry,' Talvan keeps apologising.

'Nah, you mob did your best within the system. We all thought it would be a good thing, or at least okay. The housing stuff was huge. If they went ahead with your ideas, this, this, would be …'

An eagle flies lower, inspecting the road for roadkill, but it's really just overkill that they're looking at. The road, for a few kilometres, has been painted by Aboriginal artists (not local). Bright colours, and the words 'Indigenous City: Coming 2030'.

Mum makes us pizza that night. As always I'm shocked at the state of her house, which the Federal Police moved her into until the Indigenous City Project was completed. Was this meant to be compensation for her losing her home, losing mostly everything? We sit on the floor on my nanna's blanket she made for me when I was young. It still smells good, like how things used to be.

Mum is looking too deadly with a top that she made herself and she asks me to sing a song a little bit later when we go outside around the fire and Talvan holds my hand tightly and I'm not sure if I should sing before or after I tell them both I'm catching a plane tomorrow.

2.

For my safety, and the safety of my friends, I won't be specific when I talk about where we are. Do imagine a densely populated South-East or East Asian city, where we are waiting for rain in the peak heat of July. Do imagine us smiling sometimes. If you think you recognise the identity of this city through the details of this story, it doesn't matter, as most likely by the time you read this, I and many of the people I've mentioned, who I don't identify by full name, would have moved on. You will not know this moment unless you are among us.

Here, in this place, I become a vessel for other people's stories. Maybe it is because of my queer body, muscular, long-limbed, my shaved head, facial hair? Maybe it's because of what's inside of me?

They tell me their secrets and then it is like they are forgotten, because the secrets don't define them, not really, not fully. They are defined to me by the way they eat fried eel around a table with friends, their open-mouthed laughter, the jokes they make when they are sitting comfortably. And when I have the privilege to enter their homes, I look at the water markings on the walls and what the window faces. When I invite myself into their intimacy I am missing T more than I can express in words. When people ask about her I try not to say too much as not to bring the pain closer. I miss cooking with her and her toothbrush left next to mine. It's a beautiful afternoon, the sun is easing off my shoulders, a breeze is moving through the trees, and with her here, all of this would have some sort of meaning I can't put together without her.

It's been two years, and it only gets harder. I feel very different. I miss my anchors. Last week I turned twenty-five and Mum messaged and I could not be sure if it was really her or someone who had stolen her identity as it's womba one back home. All the things we used to take for granted, like communicating with a loved one, have become unsafe. At first I kept in contact with T using a borrowed phone and a code system based on Kate Bush lyrics. Then even that became too risky.

My skin thrives in the humidity; it's just like where I'm from. I buy a handmade fan from the small store at the corner of the park, and wait. I like the nights here the most, the intense weather is milder but the streets are no less alive. I pick out my headphones from my bag, all tied up like noodles, and put on some comfort music from home, blackfella hip-hop to centre me in this strange place. When I listen to music I feel normal, like I'm not under pressure, and my personhood cannot be invaded.

I meet my friends at the pasta restaurant. This is a city that makes pasta as good as Italians. My friends are a mixed group. Some of them have escaped their own country in the Asia-Pacific because their activism no longer makes them safe. Some have lost their homes to the sea. Some are from here and have taken us in because they too know what is at stake.

N and E have come here from a close neighbour country, and are both in their early twenties. N is trans, and was almost killed online. Here he never shows his face to a screen. His family refuse to help. Despite what he's gone through, he is the most loving person I've ever met. He is always buying me ice-cream.

E is famous for her protests by body. The inside of her arms and neck are filled with handwritten words and images. She is Indigenous to a country that refuses to acknowledge the diversity of its people. She has walked the length of her nation twice but her feet are not tired.

J is eighty-five and was born here. She writes of the secrets women have carried from World War II. She is given the best seat at the table. Here is a culture that respects old people, like my culture back home.

'What is your home like?' they ask. 'Are there many koalas?'

'Yes, heaps,' I say.

'Is it okay to be gay, lesbian, trans?' For many of them are in hiding or have been persecuted in the countries they have left.

'Absolutely. Queer families are protected. Eight gender identities are acknowledged. We are very lucky. We do not have to go through the struggles you have to go through. We live in a safe place. It's a great place.'

'Where do you live?'

'In an eastern city governed by Indigenous people. You can tell who is Indigenous because they are the good-looking people.'

The table erupts into laughter, and I swallow my drink. I wonder what they would say if they knew in Australia that all media is censored. Languages other than English are prohibited to be spoken. Political artists are monitored. I wonder what they would say if I told them I thought I'd just go away for a few weeks and it would calm down and I ended up here for two years. I wonder what they would say if I told them I left for the protection of my family and friends.

There are no more koalas, only our koala ancestors are with us. In a country that used to be obsessed with mammals, only two native marsupials survive. The agile wallaby, and the ringtail possum. My Country has been sold short on so many occasions.

I can imagine their faces dropping after I finish explaining this. I know my embellished stories of Australia give them hope that things are different somewhere. I don't want to destroy that hope.

After we finish our food we'll move to The Spine, a music cafe on the other side of the lake. T knew me when I first started to string words together to a beat, drumming on her kitchen table, keeping her brothers and sisters awake. She was my first audience. I was twelve. Her mother was more supportive than mine at the time. Now my family are proud of me, and I carry them with me.

I scoop up the remaining millet on my plate. Rice faded here a little time ago. Whenever I drive out of the city I see abandoned rice fields for miles, and wild pigs have begun to reclaim these spaces. E fills my cup. I don't think beer will ever be replaced. It is protected more than water.

J and I arrive at The Spine early so we can do a sound check. I am more nervous than I expected to perform in front of her, and to translate her songs into English, which is what she has requested of me tonight. The microphone is soft. The lights are either side of my face. The owner puts her thumbs up. She comes over. 'Thank you for agreeing to play tonight.'

'How many people are coming?'

'About thirty,' she says, gesturing to the floor pillows pushed against the wall. 'People will really appreciate the chance to get together.' I thank her for creating this space, where the world-weary activists can go to collect strength and inspiration from each other. These weekly nights have been my only regular reprieve since I've been here. She passes me a hot plate of fried jellyfish chips embellished with mayonnaise, and even though I am full, I shove some in my mouth. I close my eyes and imagine what it would be like coming home to my partner. Quickly her chest will be on mine, and our lips together. I will curl into her hip and never leave again.

The shadow is wet against my forehead. The voice is a whisper. At first I think the spirit belongs here. Then I realise it has come to visit me; I have brought it here. It is from home. A woman. My great-grandmother. My heart is flooded with warmth, and my arms prickle with fear. I hold these juxtaposing feelings in one body.

I open my eyes. Groups of people have started to come in, and the lights are higher. If I wanted to talk more with my ancestor, the time has passed. I rub my nose slowly, and pinch my thigh awake.

'You are being called home,' J says.

'You saw her too?'

J does not speak further to me. She has cultural business with a woman of a similar age, R, who has entered, and walks over to her.

My name is called and I step on stage and pick up the mic from its stand. Words start to flow from my mouth and I am instantly brought back home.

When we were twelve I only listened to rap. T, though, had an obsession with Kate Bush that lasted long enough for me to have a peripheral appreciation. I remember us singing 'This Woman's Work' until our voices were hoarse. We liked

Bush until we discovered her album called *The Dreaming*. It was the first full example of cultural appropriation I understood as I received detailed explanations from my grandparents in the weeks afterwards as to why the title song had left me feeling funny. T and I fell in romantic love in our early twenties, years after my grandparents passed away. (We finally figured our feelings out when, for the first time ever, we spent time apart, as we went to different unis – yes, I still haven't graduated and she got a fast-tracked degree and a job straight out of uni.) I am grateful that they got to know her (our houses were neighbouring), and that my Aunty created a ceremony where I could come out to them. I feel them with me even more as I get older. Twelve is not an age where you can comprehend death. I threw myself into music then, and it led me on this path.

The crowd feels me. Applause soothes my nerves. I can see my friends in the crowd. When I play the next track it is my family that I'm flowing for.

While I'm sipping a beer after my set, my phone vibrates and an unknown number starts a new dialogue.

hey, they say.

hello? I reply.

I suddenly start shaking. And type another line.

The reply is immediate, a sheep emoji.

It's been so long. I ask her questions, not willing at first to believe it's really her. Before I can get my head straight, she tells me she's coming to see me.

Omg what?

just booked a flight to X for tmw morn. I'll text when I land.

Whoa omg. How did you know where I was?

Someone posted a video of you playing!

Shit.

It's okay.

No this is not good.

I'll be there soon. Your mum, Aunty, everyone's okay. We all send our love. I'll be there

T you don't know what you're doing. You'll be like me. Not able to get back home. I need to get back home.

I'll get you baby.

T's 'typing' suddenly stops. I stash my phone in my pocket. Now my legs are shaking so much I need to sit down.

I look around frantically at the faces and bodies in front of me for the person who could have been filming my performance without my knowledge. I try to spot an outstretched phone. I get up and walk among the crowd, bumping into the owner.

'What's wrong?' she says immediately. 'Can I get you another beer?'

'This is not safe. You must stop the night right now.'

'What do you mean?'

'This place is going to get raided.'

I hear a loud sound outside and I immediately duck, dropping my bottle to the ground, where it spins for a moment and then lies on its side. I expected the glass to smash. But it sits there, perfectly intact. The car has passed. No one enters. No one seizes me.

J comes to see what's happening. I let her and the owner lead me to a booth where nobody is sitting. They make me sit and hold my shoulders so I can't keep pacing anxiously.

'It's okay,' they say.

'Someone filmed me and uploaded the video. They will come for me.'

'The police will not come for that. Why do you think this?'

'They are coming.'

'We are safe here.'

I check my phone and see that all of the messages T sent have disappeared. And I don't know if she wiped them or if they were never sent.

The lights become even brighter. I can't make out a shadow or a song. I try to tell the owner and J that they are wrong. That bad things will happen here tonight. But my voice begins to falter, and to my embarrassment, I start crying. Hot tears that mix with my sweat.

J holds my arm like my grandmother, an arm of strength and brittle bone. I slowly start to breathe again.

It is a long time before I stop shaking and the room stops spinning. The owner brings me a hot calming drink, which tastes of fennel and honey, and then another. J stays with me the whole time. I soon realise that everyone has left and the music is low and we are just here, the three of us, talking softly and drinking tea. Nothing has happened tonight.

'Am I really safe?' I mumble to myself. 'Am I safer here?'

'Your ancestors are with you to protect you,' J says.

'Yeah.' I put my hands over my chest. 'Always.'

I finish the last drop of tea and put my cup down onto the table.

'Now, child, how are you getting *home*?' J asks.

I look up at her, not really knowing what she means by the question. I know what I want it to mean.

J is looking slightly over her shoulder. My great-grandmother is standing behind her and the two of them, beautiful and poised, are smiling at me.

Rodeo Girl

Michael Torres

Michael Torres is a Jabirr Jabirr man whose clan area is north of Broome to Beagle Bay in the Kimberley Region of Western Australia. Michael has worked in Indigenous affairs throughout the Kimberley and Northern Territory for many years. Michael was the winner of both the 2004 and 2005 Dymocks Northern Territory Literary Award in the Aboriginal and Torres Strait Islander Writer's section.

Billy drags himself to the rails and wipes the bulldust from his eyes. It is the fifth time Big Red has bucked him. No stockman can ride this horse for more than four seconds. He is the roughest, toughest, meanest horse in the district. Stockmen travel from faraway stations to ride this beast. Five thousand dollars prize money for the ringer who can stay on for eight seconds. It is everyone's dream to tame Big Red.

One after another, the stockmen ride Big Red and he throws them into the air. Big Red isn't going to let anyone beat him. He kicks and bucks all around the yard until the riders steady him and he curls his lips as if to say, 'Next victim.'

A young cowboy is next to ride. The gate opens and Big Red charges out, kicking and bucking. Amazingly, the young cowboy hangs onto Big Red for eight seconds. Billy is furious to be beaten by a city cowboy. He knows the boy is no stockman and wonders how he can ride.

The action is just starting and the competition is tough. The stockmen sit around and observe this new breed of cowboys. They are clean-cut, handsome and look like movie stars.

'Hey, mate, where do you come from?' asks Billy, examining their fancy clothes.

'We're the Eastern Cowboys,' replies one of the young guns.

Full-time professionals, they train for rodeos and travel the circuit, making money from rodeos. Billy is a bush stockman and determined to beat these show ponies so he organises the drovers for a showdown. The temperature tips thirty-five degrees and the hot wind blows dust over the cowboys. The stockmen are grey and dirty like the bulls they are about to ride.

Billy laughs as the bulls throw the cowboys off like ragdolls. They cannot ride the wild scrub bulls. An old scrub bull jumps, hitting the side and knocking one of the cowboys off the rails.

'I want that one,' Billy says, spitting his tobacco at the bull. The cowboys look fearful as Billy prepares to mount the meanest bull in the yard.

Billy lowers himself onto the bull's back while tightening his grip. The gate flies open and the bull charges into the arena, bucking. Billy rides it, letting his body swing with the bull's rhythm. The bull kicks high into the air, grunting and twisting its body in order to throw Billy, but Billy holds on tight, determined to beat the dusty grey beast. The siren blows after eight seconds and the crowd cheers.

No-one can get near the bull to help Billy. He holds on for his life and rides the bull until it stops bucking, then jumps off in a rolling motion, landing on his feet. The crowd cheers as Billy climbs over the rails.

'Well done, mate,' say the cowboys as they shake Billy's hand.

The stockmen congratulate Billy, sitting around him with their pannikins of tea.

'You're my hero!'

Billy looks up to see a small solidly built woman walking

towards him. The stockmen giggle as she pushes them out of the way to greet Billy.

'This is what I call a real man,' she says, shaking Billy's hand.

Billy stands motionless, not knowing what to say.

'My name's Rose. I been watchin' you all day and I reckon you win,' she says, spitting out a lump of tobacco.

'Sit down and have some tea,' Billy replies, handing her a pannikin.

They speak freely while waiting for the next event. Rose explains that she comes from a desert station.

'I ride 'em horse,' she says, sipping her tea.

The stockmen giggle, as they've never seen a woman ride. They drink more tea and tell bull stories to each other.

'I go now,' says Rose, racing over to the holding yard.

The stockmen follow her to see if she is really going to ride. Rose climbs the rails to inspect the horses before her ride. She watches as the wild horses from the ranges buck, throwing each cowboy into the dirt. Rose is the last one in line and gently slips onto her horse. The gate is flicked open before she is ready and the horse flies out, kicking everywhere, but Rose holds on as the horse bucks around in circles. The horn blows as the horse bucks her off into the dirt. Everyone cheers except the cowboys. It is the first time a woman has beaten them. They stand in shock as Rose walks past smiling. The stockmen run over and shake her hand.

'You ride better than a bloke,' says Billy, laughing aloud.

'Thank you,' says Rose, dusting off her trousers. She walks back to the stockmen's stall to talk more bull.

★

Billy throws buffalo steaks onto the hot plate while Rose prepares a damper. They've completed their events with top scores but the cowboys have one last chance to beat them. The stockmen sit back, eating their steak sandwiches, waiting for the last event. Rose plasters honey over pieces of damper and passes them to everyone.

'*You* are the best damper cook in the valley,' says Billy, licking the honey from his lips. Rose smiles. The horn blows and the crowd cheers as a cowboy flies through the air.

'Another one hits the dust,' yells Billy.

The stockmen rush over to the fence, cheering, watching their rivals do battle. Rose cheers and hugs Billy as the last cowboy hits the dirt.

'Yes, we won,' she shouts, dancing around Billy.

The stockmen join in the dancing and cheering. They accept Rose as one of their own. She is as rough as the men and smells like them. They've won the day's events and need to prepare for the next day's finals.

Camped near a creek bed not far from the rodeo grounds, the stockmen look up as Rose rides towards them. She throws her swag on the ground and dismounts. The stockmen look at each other as she positions her swag next to Billy's. Billy hands her a pannikin of tea.

'We never had a woman camp with us before,' he says, waiting for her response.

She continues unpacking her things and making herself comfortable. 'I got a jealous girlfriend, you know,' Billy says, trying to get her to move away.

'I'll tell her you protected me from them cowboys,' she says, in a determined voice.

The stockmen giggle to each other as Billy tries hopelessly to discourage her from camping with them.

'Why don't you camp with your mob?' Billy asks.

'I don't have anyone,' Rose says, shaking her head.

'Where's your man?' asks Billy.

'I don't have a man. My husband died a year ago and I travel by myself,' she says, looking up at Billy.

He feels sorry for her and can't kick her out, but still he feels nervous having a woman camp with the stockmen. The men have been working out bush for a month without female company – who knows what might happen? But she is as stubborn as a bull and does not want to leave.

Rose prepares damper and cooks kangaroo stew. The stockmen enjoy her food as they sit around the campfire telling stories.

'How long have you been riding?' asks Billy.

'I rode horses since I was twelve. I helped my father muster cattle on the station,' replies Rose proudly.

'When did you learn rodeo?' a stockman named Sam asks, through a mouthful of damper.

'My father made me ride wild horses and I rode in the rodeo when I turned eighteen,' Rose says, smiling at him.

The stockmen listen with interest, as they've never seen a female drover before.

'How old are you?' asks Billy.

'Old enough to know cheeky men,' she says, smirking.

The stockmen laugh and Billy looks down, thinking what to say next.

'Billy's twenty-five and thinks he is a teenager,' yells his cousin Mick.

They all chuckle and look to Billy for a response.

'You're as young as you feel,' says Rose, rescuing Billy from their remarks. The stockmen laugh as Rose defends Billy's pride.

'Looks like Billy's found a new girlfriend,' says Mick, grinning.

Rose smiles and looks at Billy who puts his head down, feeling shame. Rose isn't exactly his type. She's a bit on the smelly side and tough like a bloke.

'I'm going to sleep,' he says, covering his face with his hat.

The stockmen wake to the smell of bacon and eggs. Rose has been up since before daylight, cooking breakfast.

'It's good having a woman around, sure beats Billy's cooking,' Sam says, wiping the sleep from his eyes.

Billy can tell that Rose feels good that the stockmen accept her as one of them.

'You make a good camp cook,' Billy says, chewing on a piece of bacon.

'I'm proud to be with the best stockmen,' Rose replies, looking around for approval. The stockmen nod their heads, agreeing with her remark.

They walk to the rodeo grounds, excited and keen to win the final. The crowd cheers as the scruffy stockmen sign the attendance book. The cowboys sit together with their women, laughing at the stockmen. Their women are clean and dressed like actresses. They laugh and make fun of Rose.

'She looks like a man,' says one of the women, chuckling.

Rose takes no notice of their remarks as she prepares for her ride. 'They're only jealous,' says Billy, helping Rose with her harness.

'We'll show them who's boss,' says Mick, stretching his muscles.

The cowboys wear fancy clothes as if they've just come out of a Hollywood movie. The stockmen wear the clothes they slept in, stained from years of bush work. They are two different breeds brought together for one purpose, both determined to be the best. Nothing else matters to them.

The stockmen sit on the rails, watching the wild horses in the yard. The cowboys line up first as they are behind in points. The stockmen watch eagerly as they stand alongside the horses. The crowd cheers as Big Red bucks the first cowboy off his back. The stockmen watch in disbelief as the cowboys cannot last a single ride. The horses are more savage than usual.

The stockmen line up for their rides and wait for the horses to steady. The gate pulls open and Sam flies out as the horse bucks around in circles. He throws Sam off before the horn blows. Mick has the same fate. The last two to ride are Billy and Rose.

'We'll win on points anyway,' says Billy, mounting his horse.

The crowd stands and watches as the gate flings open. The horse charges out, kicking and bucking. Billy holds on, riding him like a bull. The crowd cheers as he struggles to hang on.

'Stick to him, Blue,' shouts Mick, jumping into the air. The horn blows as the horse throws Billy.

'Yes! He did it!' yells Rose, dancing around with the stockmen.

They help Billy over the fence and congratulate him. He's successfully completed all his events. The stockmen fall silent as Rose climbs onto Big Red. The crowd stands up to watch the first female to ride Big Red. Rose has waited for this moment all her life and is determined to tame the beast.

The gate pulls open and everyone cheers. Big Red flies out of the yard, kicking and bucking high. Rose sticks with him as he bucks even higher. The crowd cheers as they put on an awesome display.

'Stick to him, Rose,' yells Billy, shaking his fist.

'You got him,' Mick shouts, jumping around Billy.

The stockmen all cheer as Rose holds on. Big Red bashes into the yard as the horn blows, throwing Rose over the fence. The crowd are hushed as the stockmen run over to help her. 'She's all right,' Billy shouts, helping Rose from the hay.

The crowd cheers while the stockmen lift Rose onto their shoulders and run towards the judges. The cowboys look on in horror as Rose takes the five-thousand-dollar prize money.

'Rose is a stockwoman, not a city cowboy,' Billy shouts, holding up Rose's hand. Then the judges give Billy his five-thousand-dollar prize, shaking his hand. The stockmen cheer for their unbeatable team. They've won both the horse and bull rides. The cowboys walk off with their tails between their legs as the crowd cheers the stockmen on.

They walk back to their camp, laughing and talking about the rodeo. Mick pulls a small bottle of rum out of his back pocket. 'It's time to celebrate,' he says, unscrewing the top with his teeth. They each drink a mouthful.

'That'll wash down the dust,' Billy says, coughing.

They share the bottle around and Billy makes a toast. 'Cheers to the best stockwoman in the valley,' he cries, holding up the bottle.

They've finished the bottle by the time they reach their camp.

'I'll get some more drinks,' Sam says, mounting his horse to ride into town.

From the camp oven, Rose takes the corned beef that has been slowly cooking during the day. She removes a second camp oven full of potatoes and carrots from the coals. She slices the corned beef into pieces, placing them on a plate with the vegetables. Billy lifts the billycan, pouring tea for everyone. They sit on their swags eating and resting their aching bodies.

A dusty old drover rides into their camp.

'I'm looking for Billy Blue-tongue,' he says, spitting out a lump of tobacco.

'That's me,' Billy replies, looking surprised.

'The boss wants to talk to you about work,' the old drover tells Billy, brushing the flies away from his eye.

'No worries, mate. I'll be there in the morning,' Billy says, looking around at the others.

The drover speaks with Billy for a while before riding off. Billy is excited at the prospect of finding new work. 'We will ride to the station tomorrow,' Billy says, lying down on his swag.

The stockmen lie on their swags looking up at the stars.

'I forgot one thing,' Billy says, jumping to his feet. He hands each stockman a thousand dollars. 'This is a present for my best mates,' he says, shaking their hands.

Rose walks over to Billy and kisses him on the cheek. 'I want a man just like you,' she says, smiling gratefully.

The stockmen whistle and cheer as Billy pretends that it was nothing. The stockmen take it in turns telling stories and making fun of each other. If only trees could talk, they would reveal all the bulldust that went down that night.

Honey

Adam Thompson

Adam Thompson is an emerging Aboriginal (pakana) writer from Launceston, Tasmania. He has won several local writing awards and has been published by the *Australian Dictionary of Biography, Kill Your Darlings* and *Griffith Review.* Adam is passionate about his community and has worked for the Tasmanian Aboriginal Centre for almost twenty years, caring for Aboriginal land and heritage, and preserving community history. In addition to short fiction, Adam has written for television and performance art.

'So, Nathan, what *is* the Aboriginal word for honey?' asked Sharkey, as he swung the ute into a sharp right-hand turn.

Nathan looked left out of his open window, into the steep ravine known as the Elephant Pass. A ghostly afternoon mist clung to the ferns and trees that lined the gorge. He could feel his hair dampening from the cool air coming through the window.

'Not sure,' he replied, absently.

'Well, you're Aboriginal, aren't ya? You should know,' said Sharkey.

'Yeah, well ... I'm sure there is a word for honey, but—'

'Thought ya were going to find out for us. Wanna use the name on me label. Be a good gimmick for selling the honey, I reckon. 'Specially with the tourists.'

'Yeah, probably,' said Nathan. 'I'll look into it.'

'That'd be good. And cheers for giving us a hand moving the hives. Really need to get them on to the prickly box, now the kunzea has finished flowering.'

'Yeah, no worries.'

Nathan looked over at Sharkey and met his gaze. Sharkey

liked to make eye contact when they talked in the car. Nathan thought it was a bad habit but obliged him anyway.

'Ya know what, Nath? I was serious when I said I'd give ya the ute if ya keep helping me out like this. I reckon you've just about earned it by now.'

'Cheers, man,' said Nathan.

They hit an intersection at the base of the pass, and Sharkey turned right onto the coast highway. The ocean appeared and disappeared as the undulating road wound its way through farms and forests. They pulled into a concealed driveway, overgrown with drooping she-oaks.

'Hives are just in there,' said Sharkey, pointing into the bush. 'Might want to suit up.'

Both men got out of the vehicle. Sharkey reached into a black fish bin on the tray and scruffed two wrinkled plastic bags. He threw one to Nathan. 'This should fit you.'

Nathan stared up at the sky. It was late afternoon and there was still plenty of light, but the sky over the ocean was darkening.

'Looks like rain,' he said, as he shook out his bee suit.

Sharkey was already zipping his up. He was one of those people who did everything flat out, making his fat, saggy face and body jiggle constantly. 'Yeah, well, that's why we need to get these hives blocked up. Fast.'

They climbed over the broken wire fence and made their way through the trees to the beehives, which stood out stark white against the green and brown hues of the coastal vegetation. Only two weeks earlier, the cottonwool-like kunzea flowers had been fragrant and alive with bees. Now, their dried and shrivelled remains carpeted the ground, and the dank, piney smell of rotting she-oak needles layered the salty air.

Looking like spacemen in their white body suits and rubber gloves, the two men blocked up the hive openings with wads of crumpled catalogues, and heaved the bee boxes over the fence and onto the back of the ute. The disturbed cacophony coming from the boxes rose a few octaves as the bees were tossed about. The vibrations surged through Nathan's fingers like mild electricity, causing the muscles in his forearms to flutter. The bees that had been shut out of their hives smashed themselves into his mesh veil, trying to get to his face. Their menacing, high-pitched buzzing put him on edge.

'Man, there's some honey in these,' said Sharkey, as they shuffled the heavy hives around on the tray. 'I'll make some decent coin out of this.'

While Sharkey roped on the load, Nathan wandered down towards the sea and found a clearing surrounded by coastal wattles. He bent over and picked up a smooth stone that seemed out of place. It bore markings that he had seen before. Searching around the immediate area, he observed several more stones just like this one. He picked up another. It had a waxy sheen, and a long, serrated edge that appeared as if it was sharpened only days before. It fit snugly into the palm of his hand.

'What ya got there?' called Sharkey. He had already taken off his bee suit and was striding down towards Nathan.

'Stone tools,' replied Nathan, indicating with a nod to the scatter around their feet.

'Give it here,' said Sharkey. His pudgy hand shot out and snatched the stone from Nathan's grasp, and he held it up to the remaining sun as if to see through it.

'Trust you to find this,' said Sharkey, raising his eyebrows. He brought the stone close to his face, squinting at it while rolling it through his fingertips. 'Don't go tellin' the rest of yer mob what ya found here. Bloody ... next thing ya know there'll be a land rights claim on me honey turf.'

'It doesn't work like that,' said Nathan, suppressing a sigh. 'We can't just claim land rights anywhere that we find artefacts.' He expected a cocky remark but one didn't come. 'Anyway, all along this coast is the same. You can see where the old people camped and lived.'

'Yeah, whatever,' said Sharkey. He flicked the stone tool off into the bush and paced back towards the car. 'Let's get the fuck-off outta here. Don't worry about taking off ya suit.'

Drops of rain peppered the windscreen as Sharkey backed the ute out of the driveway, its rusty leaf springs groaning as it laboured over the potholes.

'There's some weight in her,' said Sharkey, smiling. He was in a better mood, now the hard work was almost done. All that was left was to put the hives at the new location. Sharkey got the ute up to highway speed, checking in the mirror to see how the hives were riding, then reached his hand behind Nathan's seat to extract a six-pack cooler.

'Drink?' He pulled a can of rum and Coke off the plastic ring and pointed it at Nathan.

'Got one, thanks.' Nathan took a Fanta from the cooler down by his feet, wiped the top of the can on the leg of his bee suit and opened it. It was cold and gassy, and burned the back of his parched throat. Sharkey expertly opened his drink with one hand and took a swig. He rested his rum on the seat between his legs, pulled a half-smoked cigarette from the ashtray and lit it. The ute swerved a little as he took his hands from the wheel.

'Those stone tools back there. They're not that special, ya know?' said Sharkey. He took several drags on his cigarette and, with the last one, blew a smoke ring at the windscreen.

'Well—' Nathan began.

'Growing up, me and me cousins spent all our time down at the river. We lived up at Smithton, and the river was just across the paddock from our house.' Sharkey wound down his window and flicked out the cigarette butt. In the side mirror, Nathan watched the butt explode into a shower of sparks on the slick road and spin off into the night. Sharkey shivered dramatically as the cold rain blew in, and quickly wound up the window.

'We used to skip stones a lot, and we would set shitloads of deadlines. We'd go back in the morning and check 'em before school. Always got fish – although many of 'em would be floating by the time we got to 'em. Anyway, Uncle Murray – Mum's brother – he used to come and stay with us sometimes. One day, we took him down the river and he found these stone tools – like those ones you found today, only there were heaps more of 'em.'

Sharkey finished his can and threw the empty into the back. He lit another cigarette, drew in deeply, and exhaled as he continued.

'Uncle Murray said the blackfellas used the stones to cut things because they weren't smart enough to invent knives. He said that if Grandad and the other farmers ever found stone tools on their land they would bury 'em or throw 'em in the river so that your mob couldn't come along and claim land rights.'

Nathan could sense Sharkey smiling at him, but he refused to meet his gaze. He pulled off his beanie and ran his thumbs over the rough embroidery of the Aboriginal flag.

'Anyway,' said Sharkey, 'when me uncle left, we looked all along the river and found heaps more patches of the bloody things. Hundreds of 'em – all different types, ya know? Different colours and that.'

He slowed down the ute and turned left onto the Elephant Pass road. He glanced in the rear-view mirror again to check the hives as they began the steep ascent and rounded the first few sharp bends. Satisfied the hives were sitting well, he turned back to Nathan.

'Nath, do ya know what a duck-fart is?' he asked, breaking the silence.

'No,' Nathan said. A lie – he had some idea of what it was.

Sharkey cracked a fresh can and drank half in one go. He burped loudly and blew the gassy stench towards Nathan. 'It's when ya throw a stone up into the air and it lands in the river, making a funny sound. You have to get a thin sort of stone – rounded so that ya can wrap yer finger around it. When ya throw it up into the air, ya have to get a good backspin on it. If ya throw it right, when it lands in the water, it doesn't make a splash. It makes a kind of "plop" sound. That's why it's called a duck-fart.'

Nathan, quiet, stared down at the beanie in his lap. He knew where this was going.

'Those stone tools along the river – the ones yer ancestors knocked up – they made the best duck-farts. They are like the perfect type of rock for it.' Sharkey laughed to himself and looked over at Nathan expectantly.

'Me and me cousins would have thrown thousands of them into the river, in those days. I doubt there would be any left around there now. But ya can't get away with that anymore,' he said, chuckling. 'Can ya?'

'Nuh,' was all Nathan could muster. He noticed his hands were trembling.

'Hope I'm not offending ya,' said Sharkey smugly.

Nathan shrugged, and looked back out of the window.

Sharkey slurped up the last of his drink and dropped it on the floor. He turned the wipers up a notch to combat the now-pelting rain. 'These bloody cans are going down a bit too nicely,' he said. 'Let's hope the local cop isn't out and about tonight.'

For the next few kilometres neither of them spoke, and Nathan was grateful for the peace. As they got close to the top of the pass, Sharkey grabbed another cigarette from the dash console, and put it to his mouth. He fumbled with the lighter and it fell to the floor in front of him. Nathan watched him stretch down for it, his fingers probing the dirty, worn carpet below his seat. As he dropped his head below the wheel to take a look, the ute swerved again, and this time the tray clipped the steep, rocky wall of the pass. The back end slid out, fishtailing, and Sharkey tried to correct the vehicle by swinging heavily on the wheel. The ute lost traction on the wet road, flipped onto its roof and went skidding into the guardrail on the cliff side of the road. Even from his upside-down position, Nathan could see the rail buckle and wave as they struck.

For a moment, the only sound was a hissing from the tyres or the engine and the scattering of window glass. Within seconds, though, a droning sound rose, and grew steadily louder. Nathan looked over at Sharkey, who was also hanging upside down. Sharkey's eyes were glazed over. His nose was broken and bent at an obscene angle, and his wavy, black hair was plastered across his wobbling face with blood and something else.

Honey.

The drone was turning into an angry roar. Nathan felt something dangling against the back of his neck. He reached around and felt for the hood of his bee suit and drew it over his head. His hands were shaking as he fumbled to pull the zips from the back around to the front, sealing it off.

He twisted his head to see the beehives lying scattered along the road, some piled up against the guardrail. The individual boxes had come apart and the frames were oozing their sticky, amber contents onto the asphalt. The light from the headlamps dimmed as the dazed bees took flight. Their roar was deafening. Sharkey was crying. The way his lips were drawn back from his teeth as his white, panicking eyes took in the scene before him reminded Nathan of the pony his sister had, when he was a kid.

'Oh God ... what ... shit, help me, Nathan. Ya gotta get me outta 'ere!' Sharkey screamed above the din of the bees.

Nathan released his own seatbelt and, holding on to it, eased himself down to the ute's velour ceiling. He kicked the shattered windscreen out with his foot. Bees flooded in.

'Hey, where – hey, where are ya going? You can't leave me.' Sharkey's voice had a strange calmness – a sure sign that he'd lost it.

Nathan turned back to look at him. Sharkey had given up trying to release his seatbelt and was frantically swatting at the bees attacking his face. Nathan began to crawl out of the ute and was shocked at the sight in front of him. The headlights were almost completely blacked out by the dense swarm of bees. Their frenzied movement created a breeze that Nathan could feel even through the mesh of his veil.

The crumpled ute pitched and squeaked as Sharkey thrashed in his seat. Nathan crawled through the wall of bees and out onto the road. He slip-slided his way through the honey and smashed-up wax until he reached the guardrail and pulled himself up. On his feet now and with the dim lights of the ute behind him, he stumbled up the road into the dark. As if on cue, the rain stopped. The noise of the bees grew quieter as he rounded the first bend.

With a steady hand, he unzipped the hood of his bee suit and let it slide from his head. His beanie dropped to the ground and he retrieved it, holding it to his chest. The air felt good and cool on his face. A car would come along soon.

As he walked up the dark road in a calm daze, a faint smile came to his lips. *What is the Aboriginal word for honey?*

The Healing Tree

Jared Thomas

Jared Thomas is an Indigenous author, playwright, poet, and academic. His recent releases include *Songs That Sound Like Blood* and the *Game Day* series written with NBA player Patty Mills. In 2015 his book *Calypso Summer*, winner of the 2013 black&write! Writing Fellowship, joined the International Youth Library White Raven list. Jared's writing explores the power of belonging and culture.

This one here's a real good tree. This eucalypt with the red stem. You chew on it and it keep you good all winter, boy. You chew. Taste good, iny? If you real sick you dig out these roots. See, they soft and hold lots of medicine. You mash up the root, mix it with some kawi and drink it down. When the old people used to get sick, arthritis and that, we'd boil up water and mix some of it in with 'em, in their baths, take away their aches and pains good and proper. Yep, this yirta here's a real good medicine tree, cure almost anything, even a broken heart.

Alf sat on the front porch of Cyril Lindsay House, Aboriginal Sobriety Group Hostel, looking out from the cloud of a freshly lit cigarette. Every day since arriving in Adelaide from Melbourne, Alf looked at the hills thoughtfully, wanting to be cradled by them. Alf had not returned to Adelaide or his home, Baroota, for twenty years but still he remembered his way back, the stretch of road that meets the rise of the ranges, the first glimpse of the gulf over the hill, just about every tree and turn along the way as if he had been there just yesterday.

He recalled the smell of his home, the scent of the sea and dust skipping through the saltbush. He remembered the trees, the gums and native pines sitting by the soft edges of the creek bed or contorting through the rocks and slate of the hills. Alf especially remembered his father's uses for the trees. He closed his eyes and concentrated on the aroma of lemon-scented gum, wafting from the nearby South Terrace Park Lands. In his mind's eye he could see the creek bed that he used to play in as a boy. It was full of frogs and yabbies and he was just about to grab a yabby when a ball of phlegm, sour with tobacco, hit the back of his throat and pulled his thoughts back to reality. 'Fuckin' pulyus,' muttered Alf between fits of coughing. He caught a lungful of air and then spat on a rose bush before taking another long draw on his cigarette.

Alf appreciated the mornings he spent alone on the porch as the other hostel residents slept. It was his only opportunity for peace and quiet, a glimpse of the normal life of an old man. When the boys woke they would start talking about where to score drugs, a drink, a fight, a woman. They found most of these things in the action films that hostel residents watched from morning to night. Alf thought of all the residents as boys, boys pretending to be criminals, boys finding comfort and security in stories of bank robberies they'd got away with, women they'd had, fights they'd won, made-up reputations. Alf listened and was entertained by the stories of fast cars and women, schemes, plans and robberies. He was most excited by the stories of the boys in the Aboriginal Sobriety Group Boxing Program and their dreams of title fights. Alf knew it wasn't worth preaching to the boys at the hostel about clean living – his own track record didn't exactly stand as a good example. In his youth he'd spent almost more time behind bars than out of prison and there he was, a fifty-five-year-old man, in a hostel, no home or kin to go to and without time on his side. When the boys talked about fast cars and women he just told them, 'Well, good luck if you catch them things.' Spurred on by Alf's lack of belief in their plans, the boys promised Alf that one day they'd get that fast car, the pretty woman. Alf knew he had wasted too much time dreaming about those things.

Some days Alf enjoyed playing along with the boys, telling them a few stories of his own. Alf told one young fella, Jamie, about the time he fought Lionel Rose.

'Lionel Rose was going to retire, see, but then he seen me flog three bouncers in a Kalgoorlie pub. Next thing I knew Rose's manager was there, real rich and a fancy talker he was too, like Don King. And this Don King-type fella told me that he'd give me this briefcase full of money if I fought Rose. There was a lot of money in that briefcase.'

'So what'd you say to him, Alfy, what did you say?'

'Well, a man would do anything for a drink when he's thirsty, eh, so I told 'im that if he bought me a few beers right then and there that I'd bust up Lionel Rose real bad.'

'And did ya, Alfy, did ya bust him up?'

'Well, by the time that fight-night come I was real fit. I looked Lionel in the eye like a wild tiger when I jumped in that boxing ring.'

'Then ...'

'Then what?'

'Then what did you do?'

'Then I jumped out of that boxing ring.'

'And?'

'Then I jumped on my bike and I rode all the way to Alice Springs before noticing that my chain was missing.'

'Hey, Alfy, you're full of shit!'

'Well, you're the dumb prick who believed I'd fight Lionel Rose. What you reckon I am – some crazy old bastard?'

A few days ago, after picking up a new tweed jacket from the Salvation Army shop, Alf started making his way down Hindley Street to Rundle Mall. When he saw the Exeter Hotel on Rundle Street Alf was reminded of a true story about his younger days that he could share with the hostel boys. Before deciding to enter the pub, Alf stood and watched people enter and exit feeling confused. Once he'd been served he walked out of the Exeter with a pint of lemon squash and took a seat at one of the pub's footpath tables. Alf couldn't believe the types of people who were being served inside the pub; fellas with coloured hair, women with no hair at all. Alf thought of the changes that had happened since he had last been in Adelaide, a time when dark coloured men, unless they happened to be Indian, could not be seen let alone get served at the Exeter or any other hotel for that matter.

That night Alf recounted his memory of the Exeter to the boys back at the hostel.

'I remembers when me and some fellas visited Adelaide and we ducked behind the Exeter Hotel and wrapped towels around our heads. Wobblin' our heads from side to side we walked into the hotel and said to the publican, "Two bottle of beer, thank you very much, two bottle of beer." Unawares that we were thuras, the barman handed over the grog when we gave him the bunda, see. Then me and the fellas went and got charged up at the park. True as God we were only boys but that barman thought we was real Indian men.'

Alf knew better than anyone that getting away with tricks like impersonating an Indian man to buy grog was the beginning of his end. At the age of twenty Alf was dousing himself in grog every day and thinking himself wiser than all in his drunken stupor. He was less wise as a man than he was at age ten, when he listened to his elders and took responsibility for his actions. The old people ordered Alf to stop drinking and they were prepared to exile him from his community if he didn't heed their advice. One old uncle took it upon himself to teach Alf a lesson in order to save Alf from himself.

Alf's uncle woke him up early in the morning by clanging two of the many beer bottles that were scattered around Alf's bed on the bare, hard dirt. Alf was still drunk and thirsty for water when he stirred but Alf's uncle wouldn't let Alf have a drink from his waterbag or Nhatapilka, the nearby creek. Instead Alf's uncle held his waterbag selfishly to his side and dragged Alf up Kaparinya, the hill at Port Germein, overlooking the gulf. Alf was near dead when he reached the top of the hill and as soon as he sat exhausted on the ground at the top of the hill he asked for some kawi. Alf's uncle took a long mouthful of water from his waterbag and then just stood laughing at Alf. 'Why won't you let me drink?' asked Alf. The uncle wouldn't answer Alf's question, telling him only to be quiet or else he would be punished more severely than what was already in store for him.

Alf sat on that hill for the best part of three very hot days without drinking or eating. Alf's uncle wouldn't let him sleep on the first night. Alf just had to sit there thirsty and patient, upright on the hill overlooking the ocean. In the morning, the uncle sipped from his waterbag, teasing the thirsty Alf. In the afternoon while keeping an eye on Alf, the uncle went down to the sea to swim and fish. Alf was so parched that he tilted back his head to let his sweat roll to his lips. In the evening the uncle ate his fish and drank some water in front of Alf while only sharing one cockle with him.

Alf woke wearily the next morning with his head slumped upon his chest. As the day wore on he could hear his heart thumping harder and the heat rising hotter through the earth beneath him with every breath that he drew. Noticing Alf's exhaustion, his uncle took the opportunity to sneak up to Alf and place a beer bottle in front of him before sneaking away. The uncle, out of Alf's sight, whistled to catch his attention. Alf's head lifted gingerly to see his uncle drinking from his waterbag through a haze of heat. As Alf's head slumped down to avoid torture and humiliation he caught sight of the beer bottle full of liquid in front of him. Alf lurched for the bottle and let the contents overflow into his mouth. Seconds later he dropped the bottle to the ground and began spewing.

As Alf's stomach shuddered and spew hung in streams from his mouth, his uncle walked over to him, taking the bottle that he had filled with seawater and holding it to Alf's face. The uncle played the trick another time on Alf that day and once again he drank the seawater that he thought was beer and again he spewed. Late in the night, the uncle allowed Alf three cockles and from his waterbag poured three splashes of water into Alf's cupped hands for him to drink. As Alf lay down to sleep, he listened to the water lapping against the shore and visualised waves of fresh water crashing upon his tongue. With each wave that he imagined, a tear flowed free.

Alf woke the next morning to find another beer bottle placed in front of him and his sneaky uncle standing over him and drinking greedily from his waterbag. Alf wanted to drink the contents of the bottle but instead pushed it over. Later that day, thinking that he was going to die, Alf raised his eyes to find his uncle's eyes fixed upon him and another beer bottle, full of liquid, placed before him.

'It's all right,' said his uncle, 'You can drink it, it's kawi.'

But Alf didn't believe his uncle and would not touch the beer bottle. Alf's uncle tried to convince him that the liquid within the beer bottle was safe to drink but still Alf wouldn't touch it. Eventually, feeling sorry for Alf and convinced that Alf would never again touch a beer bottle, the uncle cradled the exhausted Alf in his arms and let him drink his fill of fresh water from the waterbag.

Alf didn't drink grog again. Not for another ten years, until after the 1967 referendum. Grog was the new religion and Alf visited its church every day. He could always find his spirituality in the bottom of a glass or a can but still couldn't pick up a beer bottle. And when the old people told him to stop drinking he cheekily replied, 'I'm not drinking, I'm just sipping.'

Sick of everyone telling him what to do, Alf took off to the bright lights of Sydney and Melbourne. The only thing he found there was more drinking, crime and time inside.

Every day, Alf sits on the porch of Cyril Lindsay House and it still feels like he is inside a prison. Some days it feels like his uncle is punishing him again. Alf believes he is sitting on that hill waiting for death. His old bones ache and his lungs cry. Sometimes he listens to the stories of the boys. Sometimes they take his mind off his sickness, his heartache and dreams that just flashed by. He waits for an old friend to take him home. The old friend never comes. These days he dreams only of the yirtas, the trees. All he wants to do is chew on their leaves hungrily, hoping they'll fix his broken heart.

Glossary

Terms from the Nukunu language

Baroota	site of old Nukunu mission
bunda	money. Origins uncertain. Perhaps derived from Jamaica. Widely used in South Australia.
kawi	water
pulyu	smoke
thura	Aboriginal man
yirta	tree and also used generally for bird

Wildflower Girl

Alf Taylor

Alf Taylor is a Nyoongar writer and member of the Stolen Generation. He is the author of three collections of poetry and short stories: *Singer Songwriter*, *Winds*, and *Long Time Now* (published in Spain as *Voz del Pasado*). His memoir, *God, the Devil and Me*, was published in February 2021. He has given readings of his work at writers' festivals and other events in Australia, England, France, India, and Spain.

Grandma Polly could see the concern on her daughter's face and could see that her daughter was playing dice with the devil. But how could she stop her? Ada told her mother that she was taking her two children to the wildflower show and that she wouldn't be long away, and as usual Queenie would be the first to give her a bunch of precious flowers. Ada's only thought was the excitement of Queenie for the wildflowers. Grandma Polly nodded as she was told, in a not-sure act of bravado, that Ada would keep a lookout for the troopers or the policemen, or 'boogie men' as they were referred to by the tribe. Ada hugged her mother, and her mother sensed that *this girl is flirting with an evil that is not too far from our boundaries.*

'You'd better hurry,' she said, trying to make light of it. That evil always seemed not too far away when the Nagdu people seemed to be happy. Ada looked at Queenie, who was desperately in a rush to move. Not forgetting her love for her grandma, she called out, 'Love you, Grandma Polly.'

Polly waved as she watched her daughter and her two grandchildren heading for the wildflowers. She gave a sad smile as she saw Queenie ducking and weaving amongst the bush, with her mother and brother trying to hurry along behind.

Looking back for her mother, Queenie had to giggle, because Mum was a fair way back, trying to coax Jack who, to be quite honest, was not excited about the galaxy of flowers that awaited. He would rather have gone out and looked for bush tucker, Queenie thought.

But Grandma Polly was transfixed on the movements of Ada and her two children.

She mumbled, almost in silence, 'If anything happened to the children we'd have to blame Mother Nature for luring Queenie in.'

Innocent of the genocidal wave that was slowly drowning her people, Queenie ran through the bush in exhilarating happiness, letting her fingers flick the leaves of the young saplings as she whizzed by. Running into the cleared area, she gasped. Standing silently, still, mesmerised and in her wildflower land, she thought of Grandma Polly telling her of the beauty that appears every year about springtime. Polly would often tell all the children that they must be good Nadgu children and, once a year, if the children behaved really well, Mother Nature would send the rain down in the winter and, come the spring, the wildflowers would appear for the good Nadgu kids. And looking at what lay before her eyes, she thought, 'We must have all been good kids.'

She looked longingly over her wondrous wildflowers and knew that she had to pick enough for all the families, but not pick too much. If we pick too much or trample these pretty flowers, Grandma Polly and also Mum will rouse. Mother Nature will not let the rain fall on our Nadgu land, and there will be no display of her kindness to the Nadgu people. Looking over her beautiful wildflowers, she thought of the stories she had heard last night around a campfire, snuggled against her little sisters and listening to the elders talk, sing and play the didjeridoo. Sometimes she heard the stories being told but sometimes the elders would talk with great concern in their voices, especially when they spoke of the children in the Nadgu tongue. Words like 'hide' … 'children' … 'British Government' … 'no more you will see them'.

This would often confuse young Queenie, when sleep was about to engulf her. She would always think, before drifting off into her wildflower land, 'As long as I've got my mother, my brother and all my family and the flowers that await me I am happy.'

Ada with Jack came out of the bush and laughed at her daughter spinning around, arms outstretched either side of her, in front of the wildflowers. Mother and daughter looked over the magical carpet of flowers and little Queenie imagined that they were all laughing and smiling at her as they danced to the tune of a slight breeze. They had Queenie in a world so far away from the theft of little Aboriginal children from their mums and dads to make these little black kids like little white kids in this country they called 'Australia'. All Queenie wanted was to be around her family and around the bush.

'Hey, my big girl, looks like they knew you was comin'.'

Queenie ran to her mother, who let Jack slide down from her hip and stand on the ground. Ada put her arms around her daughter's shoulders and looked at the beautiful flowers.

Ada thought that all the seasons had been good to the Nadgu people and she knew of the hot summer they just had, the cold chilly winds that come in from Esperance, followed by the cold winter rains, which made us forever have the fires burning, and the beautiful spring weather through which the bush gave us these wildflowers.

Then gently pushing Queenie onto her back, Ada said, 'All those purty flowers are waitin' for you girl.' Queenie walked softly at first and was afraid to trample on those 'purty flowers', as her mother called them.

As long as Queenie could remember, her mother and the rest of the mothers, and even Grandma Polly, would take all the children out to the wildflowers and turn a day into a festival. Dampers would be made out in the bush. Kangaroo meat would be taken out and cooked on the hot coals. And whatever bush tucker they found in the bush they all shared: lizards, goannas, bardies and whatever bush fruit was around; in spring they were never short of the bush fruit that grew around the Fraser Ranges.

And on this particular day, thought Queenie, *It's only me, my brother and my mother. This*, she thought, *is the first time that we are alone. I wonder what kept the other families away? Never mind,* she told herself, *I will pick the flowers for all the families. I wish the other kids were here with me.*

Ada walked back to the bush and found a hollow log to sit on and was quite at ease with herself. From here she could watch Queenie picking all her flowers and could see Jack looking for bobtails. She knew that in this warm weather there'd be a lot of young bobtails out, and the family loved roasted bobtails.

With the excitement of Queenie, who seemed quite happy just picking her flowers, she had to laugh at her son Jack who was trying to kill a bobtail.

I'd better go and help him, Ada thought. *Either that bobtail is gunna bite him on the toe or he's gunna hit himself on the toe with that stick he's trying to flatten the bobtail with.*

Ada quickly got up from the log and walked to Jack, who in his frustration couldn't understand why he couldn't kill his favourite meal. Ada had to laugh at him because she had just seen one tasty meal get away before her very eyes. Picking Jack up and hugging him, she said, 'Never mind, bub, we'll get it later. I'm sure there's lot more bush tucker here.'

Looking around, she saw a quandong tree laden with its fruit, its skin quite red. It might be ready to eat. She carried Jack to the tree and could see that his eyes had lit up on seeing the quandong tree and the bobtail was the furthest thing from his mind. She was glad that the young children were taught at a young age that the bush will look after you as long as you look after the bush, and not to light fires when not the right season and to bury the bones of the animals back in the ground. It is good for the soil.

Putting Jack down, she reached up and grabbed a quandong and peeled its soft red skin from the nut and had a taste. 'Hmmm, not quite ripe but good enough to eat.'

She took a taste of a few more before getting a handful and giving them to Jack. She knew he would make short work of the quandongs, and the round nuts he would keep to play marbles with the other kids. These kids have got their own shop right out here in the bush and it doesn't cost them any money. She laughed, looking at Jack who had a big smile on his face while chomping on his quandongs.

She stepped out from the bush to look for Queenie amongst her wildflowers but there was no sign of her. She froze in disbelief. *She was there a minute ago*, she thought, and began to shout frantically.

'Queenie, Queenie. Mummy want you, bullay look out for boogie man on horses.'

She saw her daughter run out from the bushes holding onto her flowers with a big smile on her face. 'Queenie, come back to us. Run quick,' trying to control her voice, looking for her son who was poking a stick into an ants' nest a few yards away. She called to him urgently, 'Jack, run to Mummy.'

At that precise moment, Ada heard the hoofbeats upon her red soil. She froze instinctively, seeking Jack who was running towards her, his face full of fear. Then, she turned to look at Queenie who also realised something was going to happen. Fear overtook her whole body as she ran as fast as she could to her mother.

Ada was close to the hollow log she'd been sitting on and called to Jack in a controlled voice, 'Jack, run to Mummy and get in this hollow log coz policeman comin',' holding her arms out for him to run to.

Grabbing him and hiding him in the hollow log, she turned to see Queenie running towards them and she screamed as the troopers on horseback were suddenly upon her and Queenie. But what caught her eye was how the hooves had churned up so much red dust. There were three policemen on horseback but, with so much red dust around, Ada thought there were twenty horses or more because all she could see were the horses' chests and one white policeman's face on his horse. The rest of the legs were covered in red dust, and Ada could still see Queenie running towards her with her hands outstretched in front of her, flowers in each one.

For a split second, Ada thought that Queenie was going to be galloped on and screamed frantically as the horses veered away from Queenie and she was lost in the churned-up dust. 'Where are you, Queenie?' she screamed amidst the swirling redness. Ada froze to the point of near collapse as she saw Queenie step out of the thick swirling dust to give her a bunch of wildflowers. Mother and daughter let out an agonising scream. It all happened within a split second of fierce movement. But to Ada it would come to seem a slow-motion replay in her mind. Ada had just barely touched the flowers when her daughter was snatched from the ground, and the troopers held her tightly. Queenie screamed and screamed for her mother.

As the troopers rode off with the screaming child, the dust lingered high in the late morning. All Ada could see were the beautiful petals falling aimlessly to the ground, amidst the red dust.

She didn't know how long she had lain there, but she could still hear Queenie's screams and the dreaded hooves beating into the red dry soil.

Then realising she hadn't heard from Jack, she got up quickly and rushed to the hollow log, only to find it empty. Ada was on the verge of collapse again when she heard a voice in the bushes calling, 'Mummy, Mummy.'

Regaining composure, she ran into the bushes whispering fiercely, 'Stay in the bush. Mummy gunna get you.' She was relieved when she grabbed Jack who was cowering in the bushes and sobbing hysterically. Trying to quell her own sobs, she nestled him to her bosom and did her best to settle him down.

He clung to his mother and, weeping, asked, 'Will we ever see Queenie again?'

Ada sobbed, 'Wherever they take you I'm gunna find you, my little wildflower girl!'

Galah

Melanie Saward

Melanie Saward is a Meanjin-based writer and a proud descendant of the Bigambul and Wakka Wakka peoples. She was highly commended in the 2019 Calibre Essay Prize, was a 2019 featured author at Djed Press, and has been shortlisted for the David Unaipon Award twice, in 2018 and 2020.

Sunny has been thinking about the dead galah on the kerb of the Gateway Bridge every time she's passed it since she spotted it almost a month ago. The first time she saw it, its feathers were still vibrant, its body stiff. That time, she wondered about the bird's death: how had it died and fallen so perfectly on the lip of the bridge, just inches away from the steady twenty-four-hour procession of cars and trucks? And how long could it lie there?

One time she drove by and she imagined herself slowing to a stop, switching the hazard lights on, and scooting across the passenger seat. She'd reach out and rescue it from the side of the road, maybe take it to a park and leave it beneath a tree. It seemed a better place for a bird to lie dead than a grey concrete tower. But the same constant buzz of traffic over the bridge that stops the predators from picking away at the bird's carcass kept her from pulling over on her daily commute. And so, it rots away quietly, unnoticed – probably – by anyone but her.

Each day on her way to work, she's been thinking about the galah but only close to the Eagle Farm exit. She begins to think about it as she drives through the place where the toll booths used to be, and again just as the car accelerates up the crest of the bridge. She never thinks about it for long before, or long after.

It's there now as Lennon jerks the Camry's brakes on the descent down the bridge towards the airport. Sunny's forehead is pressed against the cool passenger-side window and even though her view of the galah is still just a glimpse, she sees it closer this time. The head lolling, limbs loose, muscles withered. Its wings have turned from a soft grey to a mottled, rotten brown that creeps across the dulled pink breast, as though it's been stepped on or scuffed. She lets out a snort, and Lennon glances at her.

'What?'

'The galah. We're the same,' Sunny answers. It's all she offers, and Lennon doesn't ask her to explain.

When Sunny went to the hospital yesterday, there was nothing about her that showed how broken she was. She sat in the hard plastic chairs next to people who displayed their ailments: blood-soaked cloths pressed to wounds; kids nursing ice-cream container vomit buckets; people with pale faces, red noses. The triage nurse looked her up and down, taking in her bright leggings, heavy smudged eyeliner, and bruise-free face. For the first time she hated her short, spiked hairstyle that managed to look purposefully tousled no matter whether she'd just woken up or just been raped. She felt like telling the nurse she'd come here from an after-church supper, but she was too tired to explain that church girls could wear make-up and bright clothes, and not be white, and that pastors sometimes turned out to be predators; but what would be the point?

This is why, she thought as the nurse pretended she couldn't hear her whisper the word discreetly, *girls don't report this kind of shit*.

She was almost pleased to see the row of darkening bruises on her thighs once she was in the curtained cubicle, naked beneath the hospital gown.

If Lennon was surprised to hear from her, her voice didn't betray it. She showed up with a jacket over her pyjamas, hair piled on top of her head in a messy topknot. She jumped out of the Camry and led Sunny from the bench at the hospital's pick-up area, to the passenger side of the car.

'Do you want to talk about it?' Lennon asked, after a mostly silent drive through the city back to her apartment in East Brisbane. Sunny knew Lennon understood that she wouldn't talk, so she just stared out the window. Once they were inside, Sunny waited until she was sure Lennon had gone to bed before tiptoeing to the door of the spare room and going out onto the balcony.

Lennon found her there just after sunrise, an overflowing ashtray on the table in front of her.

'Thought you'd quit when you went religious, eh?'

'I figure,' Sunny said, pressing the butt of the last cigarette against the table, 'if pastors can fuck members of their flock, then a few cigarettes aren't gonna lock me out of heaven.'

There wasn't much Lennon could say to that. She opened and closed her mouth a few times, lips smacking together.

'Thanks for answering the phone last night,' Sunny said. 'I wasn't sure if you would.'

Lennon didn't answer. Instead, she went back inside, reappearing a few minutes later, with two mugs of coffee and a new packet of cigarettes.

'Is there any point me asking what you're going to do now?' Lennon asked, as she put one of the coffees and the smokes in front of Sunny.

There was a lot she wanted to say to Lennon: thank you for making friends with me back at uni. Thanks for not ditching me when I ditched uni and friends and life for Brett. Thanks for not rolling your eyes too hard when I decided God would heal me and abandoned everything and everyone all over again.

But Sunny could also see that Lennon was ready for her to go on to her next terrible decision so that Lennon could get on with her own shiny life.

The apartment was expensive: two bedrooms, a view of the river and, in the distance, the looming shadow of the Gateway Bridge. She'd graduated uni while Sunny never went back after the summer of her first year when Brett had said, 'What's an art degree gonna do for you anyway?' over and over until she agreed with him.

Sunny smoked almost another whole cigarette before either of them spoke again.

'I fucked up,' she said. 'I really thought they could fix me.'

What she'd have liked Lennon to reply then was that maybe running from Brett to the church was a fuck-up, but it wasn't her fault that Brett had broken her and the church liked her broken. It wasn't her fault that Pastor Jay had cornered her yesterday.

But instead what Lennon said was, 'The problem, Sun, is

that you keep expecting other people will fix your problems for you. I think you should move out of that church house and go back to uni. Work hard, get back on track.'

'I didn't ask what *you* thought I should do,' Sunny said and drank the cooling, bitter dregs of her coffee. 'But you're right. I'm gonna go back to Tassie. Stay with my gran for a while.'

Lennon sighed.

'Not because I want her to fix me, I promise,' Sunny said, crossing her fingers under the table. 'Drive me to the airport?'

She feels a deep pain in her chest as they exit the bridge and she realises that if she leaves Brisbane she won't see the galah again. She feels as though its life will be gone if she doesn't remember it in those brief moments before and after she passes the body. A couple of previous times, she'd felt panicked; scared that she'd forget to look and see if it was still there. She was scared of the day when the last of its feathers would blow away and all trace of the bird that had died on the bridge would be gone.

At the airport, Lennon doesn't get out of the car at the drop-off zone. She just reaches out and touches Sunny's hand and says: 'I hope things work out better.'

Even if things do work out and Sunny somehow finds herself back in Brisbane, she knows she won't see Lennon again.

She's relieved when the plane's wing dips towards the Gateway Bridge just after take-off, as though the pilot knows she needs to hold it in her thoughts again. When the seatbelt sign is switched off, she asks the attendant for a piece of paper and pencil, and with a colouring set usually reserved for kids flying alone, she draws the galah. Not dead and greying, melting away into the concrete and steel of the bridge, but vibrant pinks and greys, wings spread, flying high; alive.

River Story

Mykaela Saunders

Mykaela Saunders is a Goori writer, teacher, and community researcher. Of Dharug and Lebanese descent, she's working-class and queer, and belongs to the Minjungbal-Nganduwul community of Tweed Heads. Mykaela began writing fiction and poetry in 2017. In 2020 she was the winner of the ABR Elizabeth Jolley Short Story Prize and the Oodgeroo Noonuccal Indigenous Poetry Prize, and shortlisted for the David Unaipon Award.

A crow-shaped shadow flies across the river. Juna knows that her daughter is coming, so the right thing to do is make her favourite feed.

Juna casts a fishing net over the river with her mind. The net drifts onto the surface, slips under the skin, and is swallowed by the water. The net descends through the deep water slowly, resting on the bed. River grass unflattens and pokes up between the spaces. Juna sings a song to attract fish to the area. The bulging tide turns the river over like a slow screw, and the net follows, one corner lifting and twisting over and over itself like a tight-rolled cigarette.

Pulling the corners of the net together, Juna tugs it back into her mind. It is heavy with water and fish. Inside her skull, she unrolls the net and five dirty silver bream, one deep charcoal catfish and a dove-grey nurse shark begin to flop and bounce. The shark bares its teeth, its black eyes not giving anything away.

She inhales the shark and catfish and smaller bream into her throat, then breathes them out with a force so sharp they fly through the walls of her skull, through the window, and splash back into the river. While they're all busy reorienting themselves, the shark eats the catfish and swims away from the haunted place.

The three remaining bream flop heavier and less frequently, embodying all the drama of dying. The exertion of gasping weighs on their bodies, the way Juna feels when she breathes in her body. The fish stop jumping, shuddering to a shivering then a stillness. She imagines this is the way her lungs will stop working inside her comatose form.

Gracey enters her mother's room. In her huge soft bed beside the window, Juna is cradled in sunlight. Gracey prowls over to the bed.

'Hey Mum,' Gracey's voice catches. 'Long time no see.'

Gracey inhales; the room is musty. She treads over to the window and opens it up to clear out her mum's sick breath circulating through the room. The river shimmers. It is very low, but at least there is some water – last time she was here it was bone dry. The skin of the water buzzes and cracks, licking the air, tasting the storm which is to come.

She sits on the bed beside her mother. Juna looks like she's asleep, sipping air and panting it out. Clear plastic tubes catch the light, drip fluid into her wrist from the machine next to the bed. She looks soft, fragile, too different. From her eyes, Gracey projects her sorrow onto her mother. Unspoken words of regret and sorry business dance in the space between their faces. The heart monitor beeps steady.

Juna's white hair has grown out in thin, soft wisps, barely hiding the skin of her scalp. Baby hairs are stuck down on her damp face, forming spit curls that frame her creased brown face in translucent waves. Her dearth of hair accentuates her fragile neck and round skull.

'Same haircut as me, aye, Mum?' Gracey's fingers brush through Juna's hair, mussing up the smooth nap and combing out moisture from the soft cotton wool. Detritus falls from her scalp like dust from an old book. Juna's hair frizzes and floats.

Juna's synapses are firing, old circuits lighting up like a refired grid. Neurons spark and spread like wildfire. Her daughter is here, in a way, but she's still feeling too sorry for herself to be present. Always so serious, that girl.

In her mind, Juna takes each fish and lays them on the hardwood bench she's set up over her left temple. She separates their bodies from their heads with her machete, fins and tails them, and shaves them down with her scaling knife. Opalescent confetti dances over the ground, sequins sticking to her arms. Her meaty hands become slick in the handling.

She slits a fish from arsehole to throat, and opens it up like a thick pink purse. The flesh is cold and sticky. She locates the dimensions of its spine and removes the entire skeleton in one go. Without its internal framework, the body is malleable in her hands. She prepares the rest of the fish, carves each body into thick fillets, forearm muscles tightening and softening with each slice. She tosses the fillets into a bowl so the meat can relax while her daughter does her thing.

Juna builds a campfire behind her eyes and sits beside it. As she waits for her daughter, she throws the fish heads into the river for Old Man Pelican.

Old Man Pelican rises over the river, lifting himself on powerful white wings, showing red and purple sinew underwing. Up he flies with an eye on the electric water and folds his wings before descent; streamlined and graceful despite his bulk, using gravity's pull on his weight to slice through the air, he bombs down into the water. He widens his jowly jaw and closes it again over his catch, excess water streaming down the sides of his beak. He chomps and swallows, skinny throat expanding and contracting to pull the fish down into his body. He soars back up, then down again for another feed, stockpiling before he will have to take refuge behind the hill, the visibility too poor for fishing.

The campfire crackles.

Gracey takes her mum's skinny hand; her skin is damp and hot. Using the sheet, she pulls Juna's body away from the encroaching sunlight, and arranges her arms and legs in a foetal position facing the window.

She picks up the framed photo on the bedside table: Juna is holding Little Grace in her lap. She's about ten years old – many years before she grew up to hate this place and leave. They were in the backyard here, fishing. Juna took this selfie, squinting and smiling into the camera. The river was fuller then, but still not as full as it should have been. Mum's and daughter's long black curls are whipping out to the side, entwined in the wind. Once upon a time, they were close.

'In the future,' says Grace, 'in the future – you used to say – we will catch fat fish, we will not have to worry about money or work or anything, and we will live a real life, just like our Old People did. We will be happy.' She looks up at Juna and smiles.

But her mum's not there. The vessel is empty, as it has been all along. Her mum has never been there. She's always been somewhere else, somewhere away from Gracey.

She pulls off her big black boots and sits on the end of the bed. Nothing has changed really, but Gracey feels lonely now she's admitted that her mum isn't here. She's alone with the idea of her, alone with nothing but an empty-fleshed reality for company.

'Please come home, Mum, from wherever you are.' She holds Juna's feet through the sheets. 'I miss you.'

Juna sprinkles a handful of spinifex seed into her grinding bowl, a hefty stone worn smooth with aeons of use, and reduces the seed to flour. She shakes it out and it drifts down lightly on the hardwood. The shiny surface turns matt with powder. She slaps the fish onto the flour and flips them to coat them, and her tough hands become powdery and silky as she handles the fillets. Her forearms turn white. Puffs of flour float up and settle on the fine black hairs.

She stands and wipes her arm across her forehead to divert the beads of sweat about to run into her eyes. The flour bonds to the sweat, becomes a paste smeared along the deep lines across her forehead. Like an ochre smear, for ceremony. She splashes oil into a frypan, holds it over the fire, and drops the fish in the hot oil, cooking quickly. She hands a plate to Gracey and slides half of the fish onto it.

'Remember, my girl,' says Juna. 'Even when the wind howls through your branches at night, and it blows right through your bones, and you've never felt so alone in your life, I want you to remember that you are my dream come true.'

Clouds converge. The glass rattles, and Gracey gets up to close the window. The wind pulls strips of water across the small surface of the river, in long thin striations, and across the wet skin the sinew warps and twists.

Gracey sits back on the bed and watches her mother for a long time. Tears drip and then rain hard. She holds Juna's feet and keens, tears swimming down her face – grieving the absence of her mum now, grieving the hard words between them in the past, grieving a never-to-exist future where they might make new memories, a future where hurt and heartache are old stormwater under a bridge, the bridge between them well-used and sturdy.

Sun on glass catches Gracey's eye. She picks up the old photo. On the day it was taken, her mum had caught a fish. After unhooking it, she made its mouth move to pretend it was talking. In an old man's voice, the fish told Gracey to always be careful with her fishing gear and to put any broken line in the bin so the birds won't become entangled. Little Grace, not a baby anymore, rolled her eyes and shook her head. Mum put the fish down. Then the fish jumped and rolled back into the water, scaring the shit out of them both, and they fell into each other wheezing and clutching their sides.

Gracey's racked with laughter, coughing and spluttering, shaking the bed. Outside, the setting sun dips under storm clouds. The skin of the muddy river gives off pale amber light. Sunlight penetrates a few inches before it's blocked by particles of mud, and the light reflects back and gets trapped in the epidermis, making it glow like honey.

~

Gracey is cooling off by the river behind the house, the river she was born in almost thirty-five years ago. Just like when she was born, the air over the bright brown water is dense with white smoke. Trees curve over the soak, and the thick air combs itself through the branches. Now, as when she was born, they're burning off the sugarcane. This means that the fish will be running up the coast; it is also almost the rainy season. All of these things are connected, then and now.

Unlike when Gracey was born, the water in the river is low.

The sun is high overhead. Sunlight streams through the pale smoke and turns the thick air golden. The smoke – sweet and ceremonial – soothes her lungs. Being here, so close to death, she remembers being born. At least, she remembers the story – her mothers' collective memory of it – which is just as good as remembering it herself.

She watches the scene of her birth unfold in the shallows of the river: her mothers and aunties are squatting in the water. The youngest woman, Juna, looks like she's swallowed the full moon. Black ash from the burning dances over the river. Juna's mum, Jenny, and Jenny's sister Liana are assisted by Juna's sister Tracey.

In the trees, crows jump and sing. They are midwives too. They hop from one branch to the next, creaky caws cheering Juna on as she pants and growls, rocking onto her haunches. The other women hold her yerrbilela, singing in comforting murmurs.

In between contractions, the women stand Juna up to prevent her skin getting waterlogged, and massage her vulva and perineum so her skin will stretch instead of tear. Juna wades over to the deeper water, howls and waddles back again. Assisted by six strong arms, she squats in the cool water and steels herself.

Soon her body contracts again. She breathes into it. Roars. Her lower body is a white-hot portal of pain. She feels like she's sitting on the sun. She crouches deeper into her squat, hunkers down into the chair made by her sister's arms for the push. The crows jump around and offer throaty screeches of encouragement.

Mum Jenny reaches down to feel Juna's opening. Everything's swollen like bloated fruit and stretched tight like a drum. Baby Grace's head is prising Juna open, wearing her vagina like a crown. Jenny feels her daughter's wiry hair encircling her grandbaby's soft hair. Juna screams into the sky. Her toes clutch mangrove roots beneath the silt, slimy and wiry and strong.

Baby Grace's head pops out, and the water beneath them reddens, then diffuses around them. The women hold Baby Grace's head and gently guide her shoulders out. Juna lies back on Liana, as the others pull Gracey out.

With another breath cycle and push from Juna, Baby Grace slides into the world and into the water, and is caught by her other mothers' hands. When the women hold her up to examine her perfection, she yowls, strong lungs expanding her tiny chest. Juna takes Baby Grace and holds her to her chest and whispers to her, crying and dazed.

'You did well, big girl,' the women congratulate Juna, their eyes shining through tears. They all hold on to her. The water is opaque with blood and tiny guppies flit around and nibble at bits of Juna's insides.

Juna's body shudders again. Sister Tracey reaches down and grabs the thick slimy cord that still connects Baby Grace to Juna. She tugs gently, and the placenta moves to plug Juna's opening. Juna breathes in. When she exhales and relaxes, her sister pulls the placenta out. It pulsates and floats in the water beside them.

Juna bites into the umbilical cord, rips the tough sinew with her teeth, and gnaws until it separates from her daughter. She lobs the placenta at the fig, and it thuds inside their varicose buttress roots. The crows jump down lightly, walk around and examine it like real sticky beaks, necks tilting this way and that. They peck at the meat, pausing to chew. More crows appear out of thin air, summoned by their own fear of missing a feed. They are noisy and chatty, flapping around and feasting on the confluence of Juna and Baby Grace.

Juna tells the crows: 'That's us you're eating there. That's our body. You mob are responsible for her now.'

When the crows finish eating they squawk and fly off, leaving black feathers behind.

Her mothers bathe Baby Grace in the muddy river and clean her caul off, then walk up the riverbank and gather around the campfire in the backyard. They oil Baby Grace's thick black curls. Her mothers' hands comb them this way and that, smoothing and mussing up the soft mossy nap. The warmth of the fire sinks into her skin and relaxes her. As her mothers paint her skin, they tell her ancient stories of resistance and triumph, and sing her myriad connections to an intricate community rooted deeply in this country in all-times.

She is passed around like the gift she is. Capable hands hold her and tickle her velvet skin, and the two younger women feed her their milk. She can taste the love flowing out from their hearts, through their nipples and into her mouth, down her throat and settling warmly in her belly.

When the women admire her fat legs, which is often, their cheekbones ripen into fat golden pears with rust-coloured blush; she reaches and tries to pluck them. Joy shines so clearly out of their eyes that it dazzles her. As the sun sets, Baby Grace sinks into the peaceful sleep of babies who are loved.

As she grows up, Baby Grace's memories of this are slowly replaced by the stories of it. But now that Gracey can see it, the intimacy of her genesis re-emerges. It floats up from the depths of the shallow river. She skims her hands over the surface of the water, remembering.

~

Nan Jenny, Aunty Trace and Old Aunt Liana are out on the veranda, sitting around the table and drinking tea.

'Gracey Galgalaw, my darling granddaughter! Come and sit down with us for five minutes, will ya? Haven't had a proper yarn since you got here,' says Nan Jenny.

'Of course, my love,' says Gracey as she hugs her nan.

'Haven't seen you for such a long time!' Nan Jenny puts her arms around her youngest grandchild.

'We missed you, bub,' says Aunty Trace, hugging Gracey.

'Missed you too,' says Gracey. She means it.

'Well, why you been staying away from us for so long then?' Old Aunt Liana says. 'It's been years since you've shown your face.'

'There's no work around here,' Gracey says, but everyone knows there's more to it than that. She squats down behind Liana, kisses her warm cheek and hugs her.

'Oh, there's work to do all right, just not work that'll earn you a fancy salary. Your mum's been having a go of it, been fighting for our river for a while now.'

'True?'

'True god,' says Aunty Trace. 'A few years after you left, she started cleaning her act up and taking her cultural responsibilities more seriously.'

'And how was that working out for everyone?' asks Gracey.

'She was doing all right, truth be told! The water's coming back,' says Nan Jenny. 'But between the stress of all the legal stuff and her drinking, well.'

'You said she'd stopped drinking,' says Grace.

'She had. But I don't think her liver ever really recovered, and she never stopped smoking. You know she started doing all that a long time ago.'

'Yep, I remember. When the river started drying up and she couldn't fish anymore.' Grace had taken off soon after. 'How come she isn't in hospital?'

'Everyone's been chipping in to keep her here. You know she hated hospitals.'

'Yep, she always said they were for sick people.'

Everyone is silent.

'She come good in the end, Gracey girl,' says Nan Jenny. 'You would've been proud.'

~

Days pass, then weeks. Gracey sits with Juna every day, talking to her and remembering.

Nan Jenny, Aunty Trace and Old Aunt Liana stay at the house too, fielding phone calls and visits, playing euchre and gossiping on the veranda.

Every morning, the nurse comes in to check on Juna, and someone or other from the community is always popping in. Gracey has lots to catch up on. Always, Juna is present, part of these connections.

Gracey prefers to be alone with her mum. When the visitors have left she selects a photo album from the heaving bookshelf and sits in the big comfy chair beside Juna's bed, curled up with a cuppa. Gracey flicks through the photos of them when they were both younger, and narrates the story of the pictures.

Sometimes Gracey puts on the community radio station and sings along to country songs, or blues and jazz. Every new song is an old gem: these are the songs they used to sing together, and she hears her mum's voice in her own. Sometimes she leaves the stereo off and sings by herself. After a while, some of the songs her mum used to sing to her in language come rolling off her tongue. Pouring out of her throat.

Visit by visit, story by story, and song by song, Gracey's grief transforms into gratitude.

~

Every afternoon, Gracey fills a bowl with water from the river. She carries the river into her mum's room and sets it down on the bedside table. She has to move all the photos and flowers and cards to make room.

She wets a soft cloth in the cool water, wrings it, then wipes her mum's face and neck and chest with the damp wash cloth, then dips it again and wipes down her arms and hands. The water becomes cloudy quickly. She rinses the cloth then wipes her mum down again, wetting and wringing and wiping and rinsing with cool water. When she is finished, she empties the water back where it belongs, thankful for another day.

Every afternoon, Juna swims in the river with her daughter.

~

Day by day, Juna's breath thins out. Gracey barely leaves her side.

One night, Gracey knows her mum is leaving. She sits on Juna's bed and cradles her tiny head in one hand, and holds her skinny hands in the other.

Juna's breathing is slower and shallower.

Gracey sings, murmurs, hums to her mother.

Juna takes her last breath in her daughter's hands.

Gracey lies down and spoons Juna's curled-up vessel, holds her in her arms the way she was held inside her belly once. She cries long and hard into her mother's empty body.

Juna is leaving. She doesn't mind. In fact, she barely understands what's happening until it's happened, because she's too busy fishing and enjoying the presence of her daughter – especially her daughter's voice, telling their stories and singing their songs. One moment Juna is there, the next she doesn't belong to her body anymore.

A high-pitched buzz surges through her and vibrates exponentially, tone and sound sharpening and accelerating second by second until they peak in intensity, and when it all becomes too much she's ejaculated from her body – a whole-being orgasm that ruptures her in spirit-shattering force. Skin emptied of herself, she escapes through her skull, campfire and fishing gear abandoned.

An immense clarity rushes through her, and strips away every single hurt and horror, leaving only the joys she'd grown and carried in her heart. She splices and separates into unfathomable directions, following the threads of everything and everyone and everywhere that had ever touched her, and so she is divided infinitely, because all that had ever touched her had also been touched by other hearts and minds and places, and so all around her country, and other creatures, and then the cosmos, she splits and peels and zooms, fracturing off in new directions with every feeling ever felt, shooting back and forth through time because all the love she ever had has manifold origins and futures.

Soon the entire known world is inadequate to hold her at the velocity she is flying, hurtling through inner and outer space faster than the speed of thought. She pings through stars and molecules and black holes and atoms and bypasses nothing, shooting at phenomenal warp speed towards the apex of the universe – the point of ultimate singularity where divisions between past, present, and future collapse into one preternatural state of fluid existence, and despite fractioning and fracturing infinitesimally, nothing of her is diluted but is restored to a wholeness of spirit by returning home to the repository of collective matter and memory – everything that ever was, is, and will be.

A new star is born in the sky, and ancestors around their campfires welcome their radiant daughter home.

*

Rainclouds gather in sympathy with Gracey's loss.

Part of Juna swims into the clouds: part of her hitches a ride back to the river in a raindrop, and part of her splashes into the room through the window and onto her daughter's face, who is still curled around her old body, and the rain mixes with Gracey's tears and sinks into her skin, trickles into capillaries, into her blood, and swims around waiting to be reborn.

~

The rains have cleared, after a downpour that lasted a week, and the river is waist-deep with water.

The ceremony is in the backyard, and the place is packed. Everyone paints up in sacred ochre gathered from the marbled seams at the foot of the mountain. In a semicircle facing the water, most people sit on woven mats. Older people sit in chairs at the back. At the front of the formation, the young ones set up speakers and a microphone.

In language Nan Jenny welcomes everybody and gives thanks to country and ancestors. A handful of the older people take their turns saying goodbye. Gracey wants to say something but she doesn't know what to say.

Aunty Trace leads the community singing her sister into the river. Gracey opens the jar and shakes the ashes in, wrist circling, her mother's remains sprinkling in a spiral. The ashes trail and melt into the muddy water, and everyone floats her away with flowers and dirt, then waters her with tears. When it is done, they stop speaking her name so that the living will no longer haunt the dead.

Everybody gets into formation to dance their farewell song. Gracey hasn't danced this dance in years. At first she is rusty, disembodied, but her muscle memory soon pulls her into the patterns of the dance. Underneath the barriers that time has created she's still a cultural girl. With her community she dances this new iteration of a ceremony that has been passed down unbroken for millennia, dancing the way her ancestors did, on the very same ground – ground that has changed so much in a short time but still retains its memory. This deep and ancient energy connects her with all the moving bodies around her, grounding them all in their home.

Afterwards, the sky bruises into purple at the horizon. In a choreographed dance of rise and fall the sun drops behind the hills as a full moon pops up across the way. Crows sing out from the trees and a pelican glides around downriver. Some of the younger people strip off and play in the river. So much of the water isn't there, but its history and its promises swirl together in the empty space.

Gracey watches at first, then joins in swimming. She can feel the old river still moving around her: a deliberate, weighted, immense body, thick and muddy, a huge snake carving out its path in the land, inscribing their songline through dusty banks. The ghost river is rebirthing, growing into its potential and ancient form from an ancestral template.

Laughing young people splash around in the long-lost water. Tiny bubbles of air and light reach Gracey's skin, and her mother's legacy attaches itself to her like a blanket and like armour.

Stepmother

SJ Norman

SJ Norman is a cross-disciplinary artist and writer, who has received numerous awards for his art, including a Sidney Myer Fellowship and an Australia Council Fellowship. His writing has won or placed in numerous literary awards, including the Judith Wright Poetry Prize and the *Kill Your Darlings* Prize for an Unpublished Manuscript. His first book, *Permafrost*, will be published by UQP.

They picked me up in their new car. It smelled of leather conditioner and perfume. Hers. French. Thick. She stunk, as my mother liked to put it, *like a fuckin' polecat*. Everything about this woman, it was made clear to me, was to be despised. Everything, especially her expensive secretions. It was Madame Rochas, I think, and I secretly liked it. It smelled like the David Jones Christmas catalogue. It smelled like the holidays.

They didn't come to the door, my mother didn't go out. Their arrival was signalled by a single, sharp beep. The car, black and shiny as a leech, sat on the cracked concrete driveway, revving its engine like it couldn't wait to get away. It didn't look right in our scrappy, wire-fenced yard. The two Rottweilers were circling, sniffing its tyres. I could see her face through the tinted windows, nervously watching the dogs, and watching me as I approached. The dogs barrelled up to me, almost slamming my knees out from under me with their joyful heft. I gave them each a nuzzle before sliding into the cream-leather embrace of the back seat. Immediately, she pulled a packet of Wet Ones out of the glove box and handed them to me.

I looked back and saw my mother's backlit figure through

the half-open side door. Hair dark and wild. Knew she'd be sucking her teeth.

My father fiddled with the stereo. Iggy Pop's 'Lust for Life' came on. This was my dad's driving jam. Track six on the *Trainspotting* soundtrack. It was actually my CD. My older brother had given it to me, at my request, for my birthday. It was perhaps a precocious choice for an eleven-year-old, but I'd seen the movie with my cousins and liked the sounds. She had seized it, seconds after I slid off the wrapping, and examined the cover before handing it to my father with a look. It was theirs now. A special soundtrack for weekend getaways in their German sports car. They showed me the moonroof. It was different to a sunroof, which was what my mother's car had. A plane of grey glass separated you from the sky.

It was chilly. They were in their smart casuals. My father in a taupe windbreaker with lots of zippers and empty pockets. She was encased in a crop coat of black rabbit fur, and more gold than usual. Dragging the tips of her red enamel fingers over the contours of a map.

I never knew how to act with them so most of the time I kept quiet. I felt like a spy behind enemy lines. My silence made them (and her, especially her) even more nervous. I was surly and antisocial. Or *withdrawn* might have been the word she used. When they spoke to me it was loud, over-the-shoulder and over-articulated. The same way I'd heard them talk to Ngoc, their Vietnamese cleaner. When they spoke to each other in my presence it was all whispers. They slipped between the two modes like ventriloquists.

The sun visor on her side was down and in the little mirror I could see her tits. *She wears them like they're on sale,* my mother had said. *Thrust to the front of the shelf. Overripe.* They were permanently festooned with gold pendants. A Buddha from Cambodia. A locket from her dead Polish mother. She'd wear up to seven at a time, all clattering and glittering in her cleavage. There would always be at least one crucifix among them: she was a proud Catholic. The size and texture of her breasts fascinated me. They'd spent a lot of summers exposed on foreign beaches, basted in Reef oil. The loosening brown crust of her décolletage contained the globes of soft tissue, like the skin of a baked dessert contains the custard. I thought that maybe breasts would be a nice thing to have. A flesh mantle to protect the heart.

'So, the big One-Two!' my father said, referring to my recent birthday. 'Almost a teenager.'

I nodded. Almost.

By this stage the CD had been changed. It was George Michael singing 'Freedom'. Another one of my father's favourite highway tunes, at least until he was made aware of the shocking truth of George Michael's sexuality, at which point that disc was quietly filed away, never to be played in the car again.

To the left there was the cold expanse of Lake George. Of all the scenery on the road to Canberra, that's the stretch that I always remember. How suddenly the void of that lake appears. It's unquiet country. To the right, a steep bluff, crowded with dark trunks of bloodwood gums and grey boulders, fringed with shivering grass. A burnt-out car body. A high fence of barbed wire. Everything unearthly silver.

There was a storm coming. When we stepped out of the car you could feel the electricity in the air. We had spent an hour following the maddening concentric loops of the Nation's

Capital before we found the turn-off to our hotel. Behind a dense hedge, it was as hushed and guarded as the embassies that surrounded it. Clocks behind the front desk indicated the time in ten different countries. The receptionist's badge glinted. It smelled the way that hotels smell.

You could hear muffled claps of thunder outside. By the time we got to our suite, heavy rain was pelting the windows. I sat on the quilted bedspread of one of the two single beds in my room. The one closest to the door, the one I'd chosen. My twin room was adjacent to their double, separated by a door that locked on their side. They had the minibar and the television. I was happy to be alone but I wanted a Snickers.

'Can I have this?' I made my way into their room and opened the minibar to find the chilled chocolate bars, lined up in size order in their creaseless wrappers. I pulled one out. 'Dad? Can I?'

She was at the window cracking the neck of a baby bottle of Gordon's, preparing a couple of G and Ts. They always had one at this time. A cigarette between her fingers, she looked at the chocolate bar in my hand, then at my father. Rolled her eyes.

My father's face contorted with pity and disgust. 'You don't need it, sweetie.'

The National Gallery, monumental ode to pebblecrete, surrounded by acres of car park. A banner unfurled down its side announced the arrival of *The Queen's Pictures*, the big midyear exhibition. A selection of the finest from the Windsor family vault would be gracing the colonies with their presence for three months.

We made our way through the galleries. The two of them walked ahead of me, her heels making a hasty racket through several rooms of Papunya canvases, seething with the colours of the desert. Eventually we reached the antechamber of the main exhibition space and found our place at the end of the queue, a heaving congregation of quiet bodies, rain-spattered jackets and damp beanies, inching down the corridor towards the exhibition entrance. There were two invigilators at the door to the gallery, one manning the grunting ticket machine, the other standing at one end of a velvet rope, unhooking it periodically to let punters through in clusters. We waited our turn. My father's arm around her waist. All of us shivering, the wet soles of our shoes streaking the floor.

The faces of angels. Virgin and Child. Monarch in profile. From the workshop of. Attributed to. Virgin and Child. A woman, carrying a man's head on a platter. Looking pleased with herself. Three strange Flemish children, dark eyes, skin like dough. Cherries and small oranges. Man with fur collar and medallions. Cleft chin, flat plane of burgundy behind. A king. A merchant. Two women and a man adoring the holy newborn. Virgin and Child. The women's hands clasped in prayer. Virgin and Child. The man's fingers, pincered, slightly camp, delivering a blessing. The baby cocks one leg up. Virgin and Child. Sometimes soft, rendered fleshy, drapery spilling from the body of Mary. Blue sky behind. Others, flat. Sideways, elongated, Byzantine. Peeling gilt, angels stuffed in the corners. The faces of angels. Virgin and Child. Psyche exposed on a rock. Two nymphs and a satyr. The worshippers of Dionysus. Women with blood in their teeth. Animal skins. Panels for the decoration of a palace interior. Albrecht Dürer. The muscular faces of the Black Forest. Death, always, stuffed in a corner. The faces of angels. The Italians with their saints and the British with their nobility. Mermaid feeding her young. There are seven of them, all boys. She has a breast for each of them. Seven breasts. All suckling. The frothing ocean. Looking pleased with herself. Virgin and Child. This one: Christ child a beefy suburban toddler. The kind of kid that would hassle the neighbour's cat. Mary's firm bicep, visible under her sleeve.

We moved from room to room, like insects devouring a carcass. I was fascinated by the portraits of European noblewomen. It was their enhanced silhouettes that held particular appeal. The rooms were chronologically ordered and every one revealed a new stage in the evolution of corsetry, beginning with the rigid triangles of the Elizabethans through to the extreme hourglass of the Victorians. I was prepubescently potato-shaped and I regretted not living in an era of stiff bodices and long skirts. I was reminded, on a daily basis, both of my girl-ness and my failure at executing girl-ness to the satisfaction of my female elders. 'Womanhood' was a yet remote and compelling proposition: among other things it seemed as though woman-ness was something you could put on and take off. It had forms that were standardised and replicable. Looking at rooms full of corsetted waists, I felt some deep and perverse relief. I wondered what it would be like to always be so upright, to be so held, to relinquish your form to that whalebone embrace?

She was walking ahead of me. Having shed her rabbit fur, her flesh was uncontained. The black bodysuit was truncated by a leather skirt, taut over the mound of her arse. She would pause every time we passed a religious icon. Sometimes going so far as to raise her hands to her mouth, overcome with emotion. My father was fond of the more vanilla Gainsboroughs and any picture with a seafaring theme. He looked at the tall ships with the same captivated longing as I looked at the Victorian silhouettes. A mutual tendency to indulge in period-themed escape fantasies is one of the few things my father and I have always had in common.

We spent almost as long in the gift shop as we did in the exhibition. They bought a framed print of a Turner for the study. I selected a couple of postcards. Andrea del Sarto's *Red Virgin*. Vincenzo Catena's *Salome* (for my mother). A Gainsborough of a woman on a swing, suspended in a green cave of summer foliage. And from the workshop of Giulio Romano, the glorious seven-titted mermaid feeding her young.

'You can't let her go swimming unsupervised, Marcus. She's a child!'

I was already in my costume, my goggles on my head, ready to tear off down the corridor in search of the hotel swimming pool. They were dressing for dinner. She was sweeping a curling iron through her fine, copper hair. I could smell it burning.

'She could swim before she could walk, darling. She'll be fine.'

She pursed her lips and turned back to the mirror. 'It's not safe. She should stay in the room.'

I saw my chance, grabbed my spare key and made a break for it. My heart was pounding. Halfway down the corridor I turned, sure she was behind me, reaching out to grab me, drag me back and lock me in.

The pool was a slender, utilitarian rectangle intended for executive lap-swimmers. I got in their way.

'This isn't a kiddy pool,' a red-faced man growled at me when I was turning somersaults in his lane. *Kiddy.* There was some malevolence in that word and the way he said it. I retreated to the edge and hung there for a while. He kept glaring at me and shaking his head.

I was always looking for new ways to be transformed by water. I wanted, so desperately, to be a water-dwelling creature, for this to be my natural habitat. I wanted to be able to breathe under the surface, to see down there as clearly as I could on land. I wanted to live a weightless life, always floating. This is the magic of swimming: it relieved me of the weight of my own flesh. In water I was something else.

I figured out that if you exhale all of the air from your lungs and hold it out, you just sink. Right to the bottom, like a stone. I did this, over and over. I wanted to see how long I could stay down there. Resting on my back, looking up at the lap swimmers as they pounded along the surface. Or creeping along the edges like a salamander.

I must have stayed in the water for three hours. The sun went down outside. The trees that crowded outside the long window gradually lost their texture. Faded to black. Until all I could see was a pane of glass with nothing but night behind it, and my own reflection, floating in the empty pool.

When I got back to the room there was a note scrawled in my father's handwriting. They expected to be back late. I should order dinner from room service.

It was almost ten o'clock before my chicken schnitzel and chips turned up at my door. I was watching a late movie. It was about a small town in Vermont or Maine or one of those picturesque and leafy American states where horror movies always seem to happen. This small town had been plagued by a series of mysterious deaths. Massacred bodies had been found in the surrounding woods. It turned out that it was the trees that were responsible. The woods were cursed, the trees came alive at night and killed anyone who happened to be wandering through them. I remember one scene: the policeman's daughter has strayed from the school dance. Some strange compulsion draws her into the woods. She goes deeper and deeper; suddenly a storm strikes out of nowhere. Her diaphanous party frock is drenched, clinging to her like a membrane. She snaps out of her trance and realises she's in a place where she doesn't belong. She panics. Runs. Can't find the path. The trees stir. Stretch out their papier-mâché limbs. Grab at her. One tears off her dress. She's screaming, running, wriggling out of their grasp. Then one long arm scoops down and lifts her off the ground. She's screaming, kicking her legs, there's mud all over her. There's a close up: the tree that's holding her extends one pointed finger. Slowly, with relish and precision, it drives this finger through the girl's torso, exits through her flat teenage navel, the music reaches a crescendo, blood spurts everywhere. She screams one more time, her body shakes, and she finally falls limp and silent.

At this point my schnitzel knocked on the door and I went to claim it. I sat cross-legged in a hotel dressing-gown, my hair still wet and smelling of chlorine, and ate, relishing every mouthful of insipid, ketchup-drenched meat. I watched the movie to the end. There were a few more deaths. There was no way of breaking the curse, which had been made by a witch who had been hanged there in the Olden Days. So they burned the forest down. But the last frame showed a tiny sapling, breaking the blackened crust of the earth, its little branches twitching.

After that came infomercials and relentless ads for phone sex. It was after midnight. I rummaged for things to amuse myself with. I got my postcards from the gallery out and looked at them. I opened the minibar a couple of times just to rest my tormented gaze on the Snickers I was not allowed to eat.

I'd noticed her toiletries bag earlier on. She'd left it gaping on the dresser. I had glimpsed into it briefly, but didn't have the courage to stick my hand in. It had sat there all night in my peripheral vision, daring me to upend its contents. In the end I couldn't resist. I pried apart its zippered maw and looked inside.

There was a bottle of Madame Rochas. I sniffed at the tip of the atomiser. That smell was her presence distilled. Suddenly she felt nearby. My stomach contracted.

There were powders, lipsticks, and frosted eyeshadows that glimmered like fish scales. The chalky, sweet smell of cosmetics. Different creams, all for specialised areas. Hand cream, foot cream, face cream, body lotion, eye cream, day cream, night cream. Ear buds and razor blades. A packet of menstrual pads.

Periods had been thoroughly explained to me but I was still mystified by the finer mechanics. Exactly how much blood were we talking about? Did it pour out like piss or was it more of a drip? How many of these things were you meant to go through in a day? I pulled one out and unfolded it. It was like a big, puffy cotton tongue. I wanted to know what it felt like to wear. Would she notice if one went missing? No, I decided. I retreated into my own room for a private experiment, making sure to leave everything exactly as I had found it.

I peeled the backing off the adhesive strip and slipped it into the gusset of my knickers. I looked in the mirror. Under the mauve cotton, there was suddenly an unnaturally large mound. I squeezed the soft bulk between my thighs. The sensation of an unfamiliar object in contact with my crotch was unexpected and compelling.

I had been acquainted with the joys of masturbation for some years by this point. As I got older my skills in this area were becoming more refined and experimental. I crawled under the covers and lay on my stomach, squeezed and contracted my legs rhythmically until I felt that release, like a rush of warmth. Every tiny muscle in the core of my body relaxed, I fell asleep.

Through the darkness, I could hear voices. On the other side of the thick wall. There was violence in their voices. Were they fighting or fucking? It was difficult to tell.

My eyes flickered open, just long enough to see the time on the clock radio. It was after four am.

The noises continued for a while. It could have been an hour or it could have been five minutes. They reached a peak and then, abruptly, fell away into silence.

I didn't hear the door open. But I remember, all of a sudden, being aware of another person in the room.

They sat down on the empty single bed next to mine. I heard the springs creak, heard the rasp of their hands on the starchy fabric of the quilt. Smells. Not the smells of my world, but of another: the hot breath of whisky and nicotine. Sweat, damp and Madame Rochas.

I could feel her presence in the room like a sudden drop in pressure. She was watching me. Willing me to open my eyes and look back at her. Perhaps she wanted someone to bear witness to the state she was in. I opened my eyes just a fraction. Through the slits I could see her dark outline. The smudged hollows of her eyes. Her lips still caught in half a snarl, her teeth underneath, her breath sifting through them. Slowly, like black silt. Her hair was wet, it hung off her scalp, clung to her neck and shoulders. That was the other smell. Rain. I could smell water and mud on her, like she'd been dredged up from the bottom of the lake.

I fastened my eyes shut and lay perfectly still, hunched in a foetal apostrophe. She kept her eyes on me. I could feel them. I even thought, at one stage, that I felt her hand reach out for me. Not touching, just hovering above the crook of my torso. As though touch were not necessary for her to draw me into the field of her body. Something moved up the length of my spine. The static charge of her presence, her slow breathing in the dark, slowly engulfed me.

I lay there, frozen in sub-wakeful awareness, for a timeless stretch. I finally heard the rasp of sheets and the creak of her body shifting on the mattress. I opened my eyes a crack and saw her dark outline in the bed next to mine.

When I woke up there was sharp winter sunlight pouring through the blinds. I looked to the bed beside me to find it empty. Perfectly made-up, as if it had never been touched.

My father was pounding on the door. 'Check-out time!' He was hollering from the adjoining room. 'Get up, lazybones.'

I shuffled past him on the way to the bathroom. He had folded everything back into his navy overnight bag. He put on his cap and his windbreaker. He looked tired.

The benches in the bathroom were totally clear. Nothing of hers or his remained. There was just my toothbrush, waiting where I'd left it. When I went to the toilet I realised I was still wearing the menstrual pad. It emerged from between my legs unmarked, the only evidence of wear being the crease that had formed down the middle, where its shape had moulded to mine. I ripped it out and threw it away. Wrapping it feverishly in tissue first.

The dresser had been cleared too. Her toiletries bag was gone. There was just my father. His overnight bag at his feet, his hands in his lap, sitting by the window.

I asked him, 'Where is she?'

He said nothing. He didn't look at me.

Wait for Me

Jasmin McGaughey

Jasmin McGaughey is a Torres Strait Islander from the Kulkalgal Nation, and African American. She currently works at black&write! as a junior editor at the State Library of Queensland while completing a Master of Philosophy in creative writing. Her story 'Wait for Me' was highly commended in the 2020 ABR Elizabeth Jolley Prize.

Swimwear can be painful. It's all tight straps, heavy tits, and red marks on your skin. My sister used to tease me by pulling the back strap of my first-ever bikini and it would spring back into my skin with a painful slap. That set didn't fit me right. And it's *painful* when they don't fit you right. People without boobs don't get the burden the fatty things can cause. Especially when it comes to swimwear.

The man standing in front of me is one of them people. He's leaning on one leg, the other is kicking mindlessly at the low-hanging rack of espadrilles. The toe of his shoe hits them and I hope he is not scuffing them up.

'She needs smaller ones,' he says, pressing his index finger towards his thumb to show he means *impossibly small*. His eyes flick down to my breasts. 'She's about your size, yeah? All your people have golden bits, aye?' He laughs at his joke, a big-bellied chuckle. 'Stuff to fill out, *here* and *here*.' His hands mime squeezing breasts and then squeezing butts.

I shrug and grimace, because he is a customer, and the customer is always right – and also because I'm not too sure what to say and I want to *avoid, avoid* and move on. I do wonder what he means by *your people*. I don't know the woman's background. His missus is dark skinned like me. So, does he mean black? Is she a Torres Strait Islander too? Cos if so, that's a stereotype I didn't realise we had.

'Smaller pieces look better, yeah?' Although his words are inflected with a questioning tone, I take them more as statements and it seems he wants me to. He's gruff. Got a three-day growth, and at the same time a stick shoved so far up his arse that it straightens his spine and pulls back his shoulders. His puppy-dog eyes are black and sweet-looking. They lower on me and his smile is reflected in them without really seeing me.

I go grab his wife – *his pretty, fuckin lady*, as he called her when they arrived – the smallest bikini we have even though the poor thing is way beyond a proper F cup. I slink the material over the door to the change room.

'*Um*,' she says and her voice cracks. 'Cool, thanks.'

'It won't fit right,' I say. And because I feel guilty about selling her something that will pull on her neck, ignite tension headaches, and eventually cause back problems, I give her the spiel that she can exchange it for something else later.

I also try one more time to pass her a beautiful structured top with an underwire and a thicker, softer strap, but he catches me on the way to the change rooms and nicks it from my hands.

He laughs at me and waggles his finger. 'Nope.'

Twenty bucks says she comes back tomorrow.

When they leave, his arm is slung around her shoulders and he holds the tiny pink bag with the tiny piece of material like it's his. I try not to vomit in the till.

The store sits on a narrow street – I think it's narrowed to persuade cars not to park in an area so exclusive and expensive, so only rich people with personal drivers will come. Not that I've ever gotten a rich person with a *driver* as a customer. The store is in line with a Hamptons kind of theme: white panelling and blue decorations. There is a lifesaver, striped white and navy, above the counter. Plenty of rope and blue glass bottles with seashells inside. There's even a diffuser with *Seaside* oil pumping silently into our air. I don't know what oils are actually mixed together to create the salty scent, but it reeks of shit if you stand too close.

Overall, the store is all very elegant, and I love being in the aircon all day, every day. I spend my time fitting people into swimsuits for their body types: pear-shaped, hourglass, square. You name it, I've been taught how to do it. Mum *tsks* when I talk about the shop too much. When I go on and on about the seamless Brazilian bottoms, or the new strapless sweetheart top. It's boring to her.

To me, it's become a sort of everything world. Do you know what I mean? It's more than just work. It's all I do, so I treat it like art, and then the world and the pain around me disappears. I love everything about that type of peace.

I pack up the store once it hits five o'clock. I'm not alone either. Sis stands there, like always – in between the rack of peach-coloured one-pieces and the straw sunhat shelf. Riley's in my mind's eye, see. Actually, she's on a completely different plane. The only way I get my sister in the flesh is if I conjure her.

She *looks* totally real. Like I could reach out and grab her hand. Almost as if I could hold her face and press it into my shoulder.

Riley walks with me as I close up the store. Like a second

shadow, she follows me to where I locked up my bike, and she sort of hovers around me when I jump on and pedal down the narrow road. I bought my bike from the university second-hand store, where the student discount is almost fifty percent off. Well, I got my friend who is an actual enrolled student there to buy it for me. My own deferred degree doesn't give me them perks yet.

The city is alive around us; fairy lights twinkle in the city trees, and cars beep and growl on the street as the orange sunlight fades. The world hums with energy, but the people occupying it don't feel very animated. Drawn faces, cold hearts, grey auras.

I look into their cars, to glimpse their lives, but don't look too long cos I don't want to make eye contact.

Bits of green flash by me, the few trees planted in our city. When I pass them, it feels like a shot of oxygen.

Riley and I arrive home by the time the sun has really started to say goodbye. I leave my bike on our tiny lawn, and huff and puff my way up our veranda steps. God, I'm unfit.

Our house isn't very grand, but it is sweet and full of warm energy. We have a small veranda that joins on to rickety steps that lead to our lawn, where the grass struggles to grow. We've got bits of everything lying around too: two broken lawnmowers, rusted toys, bikes, my aunty's car that broke down and we still haven't called the wreckers for. Next to the front door there is a pile of my aka's old magazines. Ridge, from *Bold and the Beautiful*, stares up at me when I put the key in the lock. I don't really like him. Me and Aka preferred the old fella who used to play the character, once upon a time.

Other people call my home a mess, a bloody tip even. But

to me it's usually a cocoon of safety. Nobody can get me in here.

Inside, the house smells of frying onion, ginger and garlic. And it is warm against the encroaching winter of the outside, the glow of our lights a soft yellow. It's going to be cool over the next few months, not cold cos we live north. But, still, cold enough that it'll get into Aka's bones. Climate change and all that shit.

Mum's standing with her hip leaning against the kitchen counter. Her curls are bound up and she has a wooden spoon in her hands. Despite everything we don't say, she smiles real wide when she sees me. Like her face makes creases and everything. I bend down when I pass her, and she kisses my forehead hello and her love seeps into my being. She also leaves a wet patch on my skin, but I don't wipe it away cos she's generous with her heart and I don't want to break it any more.

Home is usually where the real fun happens. My family use my house as a hub of sorts, probably cos Aka lives here. People come over all the time and, underneath the house, in a storage room, there is a collection of foam mattresses. We hoard Lipton Tea by the box, cos anyone who comes over is coming for a cuppa. Aka usually makes a syrup damper every few days too. Plenty food and plenty tea. The perfect entertaining set up. Usually there's a few more cousins or aunties and uncles living with us. But at the moment, it's just me, Mum and Aka. And even we don't feel like being here without Riley.

My bedroom door closes with a bang behind me and I flip the light on. The walls shine white, spotted with pictures, printed at Kmart. Me and Riley smiling under Cowboys white, blue and yellow football caps, our teeth too big for our brown faces. Mum in bed with Riley snuggled into the curve of her body, small head against a safe chest. A real old one with Aka Lainey on the beach, young and pulling a muscle pose while her two daughters watch. The corners of that one are fractured and faded.

My family, we have children in twos and they are always girls. *Blessed with plenty women, we are,* Dad always used to say before he fucked off somewhere after not really feeling all that blessed anymore. Now my mind's-eye Riley looks at the pictures with me. The one with her, me, Mum and Aka was always our favourite when we were kids. Our four heads take up the whole frame and, in it, you can see the threads of resemblance in our high noses, deeply black eyes and crooked smiles. On that day we had just landed on Horn Island. About to take the ferry over to TI. That memory is fresh in my mind, but really every memory of up there stands out to me.

Before I get too caught up in remembering the past lives I've had, I change out of my clothes and swap my handbag for my backpack. I pull a hoodie over my shirt, checking in the mirror that my face is pretty much undiscoverable when the hood is raised. Then I swing out of my room, ignoring the strengthening curry smell from the kitchen where Mum is.

Mum is more like me than Riley. She's usually always meeting up with friends and talks way too much in polite conversations. Whenever she's asked 'how you going?' as a hello, she never just says fine. Mum will go on and on about her day and everything that's happening in her life. Me and her are both chatterboxes. She's not like that so much at the moment though. These days she just says fine cos she doesn't wanna make anyone uncomfortable with all her grief.

Mum has her back to me, luckily, and I make it out the front door without a comment.

'Aye!' Aka Lai's voice cuts through my heart and shocks my system.

I get my breathing under control before turning to face her.

She sits on the veranda, beginning a card game on the fold-out table I got her from Bunnings. She places plastic tablecloths over it and, when it rains, she puts towels on top, so the *plastic* tablecloths won't get wet. I don't understand half the things she does.

I wander up close to her and lean against the front door frame.

'Wanem wrong, Kala?' she says, while keeping her eyes glued to her game. Solitaire maybe?

I breathe out slowly, a thumping going off wildly inside me. Riley moves closer and her hand brushes up against mine. My skin gets a tingling feeling, like colourful fireworks buzzing through my veins. But it doesn't feel like a real hand touching mine.

It's just Riley, doing her best to persuade me to stay here.

I smile at my grandmother and convince myself I am being genuine.

Aka Lai's mouth twitches and my stomach muscles tighten in response. It's like there's this energy between us. I can almost see the red vines of our auras tying together. Connecting my mind with my aka's. It pulses with knowledge. Warmth vibrates from it. She knows me. She knows something about what we've hardly discussed.

She swallows and the lines in her face deepen. Beautiful.

Aka Lai came from TI when my mum was a kid. She and my athe held two suitcases each and lived in a house full of his relatives. She got a job as a receptionist at a doctor's office and still works there now. I reckon she wants to return home but couldn't bear to be far away from us.

This place is the next best thing anyways, since there's plenty island people here.

'I mina love you,' she says slow one, glancing up at me.

My throat immediately gets choked up. Some part of me is real touched by this small admission, which *of course* I knew. I know it as well as I know I breathe air to live.

'I love you too.'

She nods and returns her eyes to the cards in front of her.

I sigh and reach back towards the front door to turn the porch light on. 'You shouldn't be playing cards in the dark, Aka.'

The harsh yellow illuminates her small body suddenly, like she's an angel. Her white hair, a halo. I don't feel unsteady or uncertain anymore. The sight of her makes me sure.

'Ah, mata quick game here,' she answers.

'Yeah, sure.' Although I feel unwavering in my nightly task, I am hesitant to leave the comfort of her presence. She senses it and looks up at me.

'Wanem?' she asks, eyes narrowing again.

'Just ... everything.' My inability to express what I really mean is hereditary.

She nods though, because words aren't always necessary to express feelings.

'Wa, I sabe,' she says.

I sniff the stinging in my nose away and shake my head a few times to clear my eyes. I lean over and kiss her cheek, soft and sweet smelling. As I pull away, her hand grabs my wrist and she keeps me close. She lifts herself further upright in her chair and touches our foreheads together. I squeeze my eyes shut and accept the love.

After a moment she releases me, and the air gets caught in the back of my throat.

I can feel Riley vibrating to my side. She wants this too. She wants to reach out and have our aka hold her, kiss her, and make everything okay.

I stand straight and spot my mum looking at us through the window. Her brows are creased and her mouth open as if she is about to call out for me to come back inside. She splays her hands out with a shrug of her shoulders. *Where are you going?*

I'm surprised she hasn't soldered a tracking bracelet to my wrist at this point. I kinda want to do the same to her and Aka.

Friends, I mouth back at her.

Her frown deepens but she doesn't beckon me inside, nor does she come to me and drag me back to my room. Part of me longs to be taken care of like I'm a child again. For that simplicity. Before Mum can call me inside and treat me like that, I lift my hand in a wave.

'You right, ah?' Aka whispers, as I lift my backpack up higher on my shoulders.

I shake my head and then nod, contradicting myself. 'Wa,' I say. 'Yawo.'

Mum presses her hand to the glass. Aka jerks her head in goodbye and, as I am bounding down the steps and lifting up my bike, I feel them both watching my back. Riley follows, gliding down from our veranda like sand falling from hands. We go off into the night, the two of us, like we used to when it didn't require a real effort just to see her, me on my bike and her dragged along by my mind.

The car park is dimly lit. Still. Council haven't learnt a thing from my letters. It's empty, but for a lone white sedan that has police tape telling us the cops know about it. The car is creepy, but I reckon I might be freaked out more if I turned up one night and it wasn't there. It's part of the setting now.

Riley shivers needlessly beside me. She's not cold. Just wants my attention.

My tongue touches my lips and I taste salt. Gentle rolling waves breach through the nothingness towards me. They aren't real waves, not like down south. Just baby ones that want to be heard and yet you must strain to hear them. I can also make out the whistle of sand dancing down on the beach. No gulls, no other people. No sound of life other than that of the land.

Mum and I reckon we live near the beaches cos we are saltwater people, and since we don't live on the islands, we need to be connected to the water in any way we can. When I was little, we used to live right on the beach and the lapping of the ocean would lull me to sleep. Maybe that's why I work in a swimwear store!

I've been coming to the beachside car park here on the northside for too many nights to count now. It's a relatively small beach that stretches just under a kay. It's not very busy, with only one corner store and one fish and chip shop. There aren't any houses along it either, aren't many people to bear witness to you. Homes are set back a block cos there was supposed to be big flash apartments built, but not even the digging got underway before the company planning it went bankrupt.

I go to my spot, the wooden steps that lead you up onto the sandy dune before you tumble down to the water. The stinger-, crocodile-, and shark-infested water.

The steps are tucked in between plants and long grass. And there are wood splinters in certain places so I gotta be careful where I place my din. When I sit on them, I know no-one else can see me, even if they drive past or park their car directly in front of me. I know because Riley couldn't see him.

Whenever she or I used to walk the beachside way home, we'd always hold our keys in between our knuckles. Mum joked that we should carry pepper spray, and we laughed about not knowing where to even buy it. I can make it myself now – I googled it: chopped chilli, garlic, oil and a dash of vinegar. Images of mine and Riley's practice jabs and right hooks flash with a bitter taste in my mouth now. Giggling play fights are distant memories.

I settle onto the steps and open my backpack. Reaching in, I pull out the metal; it's cold against my palm, but the rest of me feels flushed. Speckled heat across my cheeks.

I roll it in my hands – it's the length of my forearm and hand together. Rust has covered the two ends and it crumbles a little under my touch.

Time passes in a different way here. It's like it continues on around me, while I wait, paused. Really, I'm not even sure I know what will happen on these nights I come. I don't even know if I'd be able to stand up against the scary something that I know *could* happen.

Riley stations herself behind me. She stands, or hovers, and watches over my head like a lighthouse – waiting to protect me. Not that she could.

She is quiet, but I can feel her impatience and frustration with me. If I had enough imagination to make her talk, she'd tell me to go on and piss off outta here. I would listen if she could tell me that. Honest.

Now that I'm sitting still, I can hear even more undercurrents of life on the beach. A rustle here, a crunch of sand under feet there? It all sends my ears perking up, and I feel like a dog listening out for the words *walk* or *park*. Except it's not excitement in my tummy. It is fear and an unending wave of fury.

I jump when a streetlight near the car park, usually broken, flickers on. A shadow appears under the light. My grip tightens around the tool in my hands and I grit my teeth.

The shadow moves towards me.

Big shoulders.

Thick body.

My heart stutters and my fingers and toes turn cold.

It freezes, just at the edge of the lamp's light.

We stare at each other, me and this creature.

And then I blink, and it is gone.

I let out a breath and realise my heart is beating too fast. Did Riley's heart beat this fast? I look up at her, but her jaw is locked, and she won't glance down at me. She's very mad.

It must be close to seven or eight pm by the time I lose my nerve, like usual. The dark gets a new meaning once a certain number of minutes click by. Maybe cos curfew used to be eight-thirty for me and Riley when we were kids in school, and now I can't bring myself to break the habit for long. But I think knowing nobody could be possibly driving this way now is what makes me frightened even more.

My limbs feel like they drag with disappointment as I move across the sandy grass and then onto the rough gravel. Shadows of my body stretch over my path as I walk back across the car park, putting the metal something back into my bag and shouldering the pack. Shouldering the yuckiness that holds my heart.

I find my bike and get on, making sure my Riley isn't too far away.

The hospital is like a beacon compared to the darkness at the beach. I had to stash my bike behind a bush and a frangipani tree and then luckily wait only five minutes for the bus. I would have called an Uber, but these days I'm a little low on funds. Besides travelling across the city, with no-one but me, the driver and my sister, was comforting, and I almost fell asleep. But when we stopped outside the hospital, the driver barked at me to *get the fuck off.*

It is right across the road from the Esplanade. I suppose that makes for some interesting scenery, and maybe being by the water and looking out at the sea is helpful *emotionally* to the patients. I like to believe it is.

I walk right in the front doors, and my sister follows me. She keeps glancing over her shoulders, very nervous. I would guess she doesn't like to come to the hospital – it's kinda creepy.

Visiting hours will be over in fifteen minutes so I speedwalk and sweat gathers under my pits. I'm nervous too.

The lobby is noticeably empty. I do see one woman alone at

the lobby café. She is slouched in on herself, holding her head in her hands. Her aura is crying out of her body, greys and silvers dripping like diamonds onto the polished floors. Two older folk clutch each other by the stairs and their intensity scares me so much I take the lift.

Nurses pass me and, even though I don't know them, even though I am a stranger here, they give me welcoming nods and smiles. They're a godsend, Mum reckons.

The room is in the corner and, just like I've been told, she has it all to herself.

Riley's bed is in the middle, facing the TV Mum says is never put on. Riley always hated regular TV; she only liked Netflix or Stan. American shows she could binge in one weekend. She would always say *Home and Away* and *Neighbours*, our mum's and Aka's favourite shows, were vapid. I don't know why she'd use that word, probably cos she thought we wouldn't know what it meant. Mum and Aka Lai would just scoff. I'd roll my eyes and point out when the actors were wearing the brand of swimwear I sold.

Her eyes are closed, and her hair is braided on one side. Mum does it, with the help of the nurses every so often. They brush it out and run oil through the strands to make it strong for when she comes back to us properly.

I stand close to the bed and put my hands on the blanket covering her.

She has become a reduced version of what she once was. It hurts to look at her now, but I owe her that much. She is surely hurting more than me.

I look at my mind's-eye Riley who has followed me around all evening and is standing next to me now. She's fuller, brighter than the real Riley. The brown of her hair is deeper, her cheeks rounder, and her eyes glint.

She's watching me, and I expect her to disappear, cos surely seeing this real Riley in person is confusing and worrying to her. Technically, she should dissipate back into the atmosphere again, back into the real Riley. Or fizzle back into my mind, I suppose.

The Riley beside me doesn't fade away though. She blurs and for a moment I think she might speak. She's never spoken before.

Her hair lifts and stretches up, like when you rub a balloon on your arm and the static electricity sends the strands on your arm upright. There's a light flickering in her eyes. She's *alive* with emotion.

I stare at her and she stares back.

But I can't take it anymore, because this means something, and it might be something I'm not ready for. I squeeze everything shut. Block out the noise. Block out the sights. My hands tighten on the blanket that is covering my very *real* sister. The cotton feels rough and heavy, jolting and comforting. It's all too confusing to allow my senses to acknowledge.

My knees buckle and the sensation of falling extends to my heart and my mind. I sink down further and press my face into Riley's belly. My arms go around her, and *I won't think* about what's happening around us, to us. To her.

I'll never, ever leave her.

Split

Cassie Lynch

Cassie Lynch is a writer and researcher living in Boorloo/Perth. She is a descendant of the Noongar people and belongs to the beaches on the south coast of Western Australia. She has a PhD in Creative Writing that explores Aboriginal memory of ice ages and sea-level rise. She is a student of the Noongar language and is the co-founder of the Woylie Project. Her writing has been featured in Perth Festival, Fremantle Arts Centre, City of Perth, *Westerly*, Artsource, and Brio Books.

A black swan glides across the surface of the river and lands with a soft splash near a batch of reeds. It floats through the base of a semi-solid statue of a European man, his gaze fixed on the horizon. The swan cranes its neck and grooms under its wing.

Did you come here looking for Water?

I'm standing in Perth, a city located on the banks of a river on the south-west coast of the Australian continent. I'm in the central business district, on a long, wide road with deep kerbs, surrounded by a rectangular gorge of skyscrapers. I am walking north and in between the glass and concrete buildings I see glimpses of the Swan River, a blue snaking body of water.

It is the afternoon. Office workers hurry past carrying document wallets and laptop bags. Couriers push trolleys stacked with boxes. Road crews peer into excavated cable tunnels. Charity volunteers shake tins. Thousands of pairs of feet create a dull patter against the rumble of buses and cars and construction. The glass canyon collects the sounds of rubber hitting hard surfaces and bounces them around.

A tiger snake emerges from a storm drain and swims across the surface of the water. A scooter drives right through its body

169

as the striped serpent makes its way towards a clump of bulrushes. The snake's waving swim is undisturbed. It disappears into the fringe of green.

Beyond the buildings the river is mild-mannered. The Swan River, so named three hundred years ago by a Dutch explorer, is a creation of the new people, the settlers from over the seas. They infilled the swamps that were here, turning riverland into parkland. They gave the river new banks, new borders. They dammed the tributaries coming down from the eastern hills, changing the flow. The Swan River is a bound river. But there is an older river within. The Bilya. This river is the sweet water body of the creator serpent – the Wagyl, as it is known in the first language of this place.

The main banking institutions are here on this street, and the mining companies. There is prestige attached to possessing the best view of the Swan River. Settlers manufactured dry land to stake their buildings into. It is only a temporary possession though. A recent occupation.

I walk towards the tallest building on the street and enter its broad plaza filled with dining tables and benches. An osprey dives from above and plucks a wriggling salmon from between two suited men eating their lunch at the tables. A cormorant shrieks from its perch in a swamp banksia growing through the centre of the feature water fountain. The tips of melaleuca flowers dip in and out of latte froth, moving on the breeze. Across the expensive pavers are glass doors that lead into the building. I can see that there are bulrushes in the foyer.

A thread catches my eye and I instinctively brush it away from my face. I can barely feel it on my fingertips. A spiderweb.

I walk around the side of the building and descend a concrete ramp to the underground carpark. I lean against the wall as a dirty van trundles up from the depths. I arrive at the basement, climb up on a sedan and settle on its roof. The water here comes to halfway up the windshields of the cars parked. I sit. A rainbow bee-eater flits past my face and lands on the branch of a wattle tree growing from within a ticket machine. The top of the tree reaches through the concrete ceiling above, and the bee-eater disappears up into its branches and through the roof. I look out across the car park, my eyes searching. I see it. A spray of air and water. A curved dorsal fin breaking the surface. This basement car park is a favourite spot for dolphins. It has become a favourite spot of mine.

I slide off the car and into the water. It doesn't penetrate though. I am as dry as those who do not notice the dolphins or the snakes. I walk back up the ramp and onto the street. I stand back and admire the swamp that occupies Perth city. The road outside is an undulating stream. The pavement is taken over by sedges and reeds. The buildings are pierced by banksias, paperbarks and gums.

Did you come here seeking Air?

Beneath my feet, deep under Perth, is a scar. Hundreds of millions of years ago, the creator serpent split the billion-year-old crust in two. Half the continent was shorn away, leaving a bubbling sea of molten rock in its wake. Such were the brutal beginnings of Noongar Country.

Noongar land is a place of abundance, spirit, and culture. Noongar people cared for it before the settlers came. Noongar people continue to care for it.

The ocean of lava cooled leaving a broad basin of black rock attached to the new edge of the Australian continent. In the distance, the Indian plate was making its way north where it would crash into Asia and push up the Himalayas. The basin left behind was fifteen kilometres deep and thousands of kilometres long. The Wagyl got about creating.

The creator serpent is a Rivermaker and Rainlord. It wore down the mountains of inland Australia and washed the broken pieces into the scorched basin. Layer upon layer of fragmented earth was laid down, forming bands of sandstone and shale. The serpent pushed up hills and sank swamplands, and beaches were crafted from the skeletal remains of ancient sea creatures. The Wagyl's watery body embedded itself in the landscape, bringing life and health to this new creation. A dusting of soil and plant matter settled delicately across the surface. This is the Swan Coastal Plain, a Riverland, built as a paradise for the humans and animals to come.

The memory of split earth remains, though. The Darling Scarp, the mountain chain to the east of Perth that runs parallel to the ocean, is the thousand-kilometre-long surface expression of where the Indian plate sheared off. The land remembers the violence that begot it.

Today this rich and storied Country lives under bitumen, brick and grass. Skyscrapers are the new signifiers of a history of violence.

I come to stand next to the bronze statues of kangaroos set in front of a local government building. Two drink from an artificial pool. The settler has become water-maker. Three kangaroos are bounding away, their backs to the pool and the Swan River, fleeing both actual and manufactured water.

I lean in and inspect the dark expression of the large male. He is looking east – to the Scarp perhaps? I run my fingers along its neck and a glistening thread emerges from my palm. I break it off and let it drift away on the breeze.

Settlers will say that they brought science, technology and worldly culture to the shores of this wild country. Marvels. Advancements. Shakespeare. The wheel. And they did.

But they also brought savagery to Noongar Country. Slavery. Poverty. Incarceration. Massacre.

I step out of the way of a group of teenagers in private-school uniforms who are laughing as they walk. A family of ducks float through my legs.

There is another import to Noongar Country that has gone largely unnoticed.

Time.

Settlers are manufacturers of their own particular Time. European Time. Chronological Time. Linear Time. Biblical Time. The kind of Time that began not long ago, is happening now, and will end one day. This ancient continent has its own: Deep Time.

Noongar mob are pattern-thinkers and cycle-watchers. We remember the last Ice Age, tell stories of the Cold Times. Deep Time is a stone dropped in a pond and we read the ripples. This Country remembers what it was. It remembers everything that it has ever been. Settler Time overwhelmed us, but Deep Time endures.

Geologists can see what the creator serpent did, can read part of that story in the rocks. Ancient continent, they say. Blown flat by Time.

The sun is on its way down. The sky is pale blue with

grey-pink clouds, reflecting in the river. Near my feet a tortoise with a thick carpet of shaggy moss on its shell is making its way past a traffic cone to its secret home somewhere within the walls of a restored church.

The streets are filling with people leaving work for home. Thousands of bodies. They are sliding through the swamp undampened. They traverse like cross-cosmic travellers in spacesuits walking on a foreign planet, carrying with them the atmosphere of their place of origin.

Anthropocene Air.

Threads continue to shed off me and float away on the breeze. The swamp water around my legs is feeling colder.

This Anthropocene Air was brought to Noongar Country from the European civilisations across the seas. It travelled with them on the ships, in the lungs of convicts, soldiers and settlers, trapped in their clothes, clinging to objects they brought with them. Like a second skin, an Air around them, a buffer between the minds and bodies of settlers and the Deep Time of Noongar Country. After more than two hundred years this coating of Air has survived. Parents breathe it into their infants born here, English language generates and replenishes it, children absorb it from art, music and stories. Anthropocene Air clumps together in cities and communities, bolstering it, reinforcing it.

This Air is around our feet, our hands, our eyes, our tongues. We walk on Air, a cushion of resistance between the soles of our feet and the soil of Noongar Country. A cloud that distorts and bends Time around us, keeping us in the quicker experience of Settler Time, and blocking out the cyclical Deep Time, the kind of Time that can split continents, raise mountains and fill oceans.

In this suit of Air we slide across Noongar Country. Never settling in, never sinking down.

I pull something like a clump of spiderwebs away from my arm. I let it go and see a shiny patch of transparent film float down to the swamp water.

Something has happened to my Anthropocene Air.

A dorsal fin breaks the surface of the road-river in front of me. Its tip points towards the sky, unlike the curved fins of the dolphins of the basement carpark. I leave the bronze kangaroos and walk a few steps down towards a street corner. I turn back to see that the fin, rudder-like and with compass accuracy, has zeroed in on me. I step off the kerb, jellyfish fleeing from my path, and a cold sensation creeps up my legs. I hurry across the road and step up onto the next street corner. I look back. The fin is following.

I quicken my pace and weave between people leaving work. I feel safe in the thick throng of humans. My legs are feeling heavy and cold.

I turn and a mother pushing a pram is about to run me over. I bring my hand up to stop the pram crashing into me but my hands touch nothing, the mother walks right through me. I am frozen on the spot, my eyes darting around.

The light changes around me. The skyscrapers are losing their solidity. The golden late-afternoon sun now filters straight through them, illuminating all the water around me. Coldness creeps up my legs and I look down and see that I am damp to my knees. The pedestrians walking past look like ghosts; light passes through their heads, obliterating their facial features. The outline of a suited man approaches me and my eyes pass through his eyes as we occupy the same space, impossibly, for a moment.

My hair stands on end. I glance back over my shoulder and see the dorsal fin bearing down on me again. I turn and run. The swamp water is dragging against my legs. I can still feel pavement under my feet but the reeds are dragging me back. Pieces of diaphanous Air are peeling off from my chest like rotted rags. I keep running and splashing among the spectres of citizens. I reach another street corner and I leap off the kerb. When I land there is no road beneath and I sink like a stone into cold water. I reach up for a handhold but my body weight plunges me deeply. I sense a dark shape moving overhead and my fingertips graze the underside of a smooth, slick belly. Panicked, I kick my legs and search for the surface. The water is holding me down, like the coils of a snake around my limbs.

Water and Air.

I break the surface and look around wildly. I see the cliffs of Kings Park, rising high above. I turn and the bank of the South Perth foreshore is far behind me.

I must be in the Swan River.

No.

There are no buildings. No luxury apartments on the foreshore. No skyscrapers piercing the river banks.

I swim towards a rocky spit covered in reeds. My feet find a foothold and I climb out of the water, coming to stand on a sandy islet. I glance around and the shorelines are different; they are fuller, deeper. The Swan River that I know isn't present. This is the Bilya.

The city isn't there. Just swamp, streams, sandhills and limestone. Banksia, paperbark, melaleuca and gum. Swans, herons, pelicans and gulls. It's very quiet. The evening sky above is dappled with pink and violet clouds. There is no sign of people around. I am alone.

I look down at my hands and they are draped with a barely perceptible translucent coating. I pinch it with my fingers but it's too fine to get a hold of. Shreds of this material hang all over my body. I move my fingers to my mouth and push strands away from my lips. I breathe in deeply.

A heron walks past in the reeds, long-legged and soft-footed, looking for crabs. The water gives off light where it is disturbed.

A ragged piece of Air is hanging from my elbow and I wonder at it. How did it become so flimsy? I crouch and dip the edge into the water. It fizzes slightly. I pull it out and the transparent fabric has frayed out into threads.

Riverwater can split rock, dig basins, wear away mountains.

The water was there, patiently wearing away my suit of Anthropocene Air. The lakes and swamps seep through. I look around and see that there is no dry land in Deep Time Perth. The landscape is a pervasive memory of saturation. The reclaimed earth that the skyscrapers occupy is only temporary, ephemeral even. It wasn't there in the past and it won't be there in the future.

I see a dolphin pod chasing bream out in the open.

Do I want roads and parks here again? My grandmother's culture was bitumined and concreted and bricked and grassed. My grandfather's culture brought Anthropocene Air from across the sea. Perhaps all my life I have been marooned on unnatural dry land along with everyone who settled here. Like sea creatures washed onto a rock, gasping for life, and the Deep Time memory of the river flowed over us, invisible, keeping us alive. Held between Water and Air.

I stand on the rocky shore of the Bilya, the ecstatic and unbound body of the Wagyl. The water is glinting in a way that I've never seen before. Reds, blues, greens and yellows are bouncing across the surface. An invitation from the creator serpent. Jump back into the water. I will rid you of that suit of Air for good.

Evening in Deep Time Perth is settling in. The amber light from the sunken sun fades and the sky is a deep indigo. Out of the corner of my eye I see a flicker. I turn and face where the city was and something is glinting there, something in the Air maybe, but I can't make it out. I turn and look up at Kings Park, no, Kaarta Gar-up, and there are shadows dancing between the trees. I run my hands across my eyes and I can feel the shreds of my suit of Air. With a slow movement I brush the remaining strands from my face and look again.

My vision is overcome with rainbow prisms and I blink rapidly. Slightly nauseated, I look up at Kaarta Gar-up and see the glow of campfires dotting the clifftop. People. Noongar mob. The light of my ancestors shines through the vast memory of Deep Time.

Not so alone.

I look back at the swamps of Perth and see that there are pinpoints of light there too. In the Air. Hanging in nothing. Hovering lights in columns, up and down and across. They have a grid-like arrangement, strange against the natural splendour. I realise what they are. The lit-up windows of the city pierce through to glow over the Deep Time river landscape.

Did you come here seeking Light?

I settle onto a rock. Far beneath where I sit, under layers and layers of broken pieces of long-dead mountains, is a split landscape. In Settler Time it has healed and changed into the paradise that is Noongar Country. But in Deep Time that split echoes, and echoes, and echoes.

Dreamers

Melissa Lucashenko

Melissa Lucashenko is a Goorie author of Bundjalung and European heritage. Her first novel, *Steam Pigs*, was published in 1997 and her work has received many awards. Her sixth novel, *Too Much Lip*, won the 2019 Miles Franklin Literary Award. Melissa is a Walkley Award winner for her non-fiction, and a founding member of human rights organisation Sisters Inside.

'Gimme an axe.'

The woman blurted this order across the formica counter. When the shopkeeper turned and saw her brimming eyes he took a hasty step backward. His rancid half-smile, insincere to begin with, vanished into the gloomy corners of the store. It was still very early. Outside, tucked beneath a ragged hibiscus bush, a hen cawed a single doubtful note. Inside was nothing but this black girl and her highly irregular demand.

The woman's voice rose an octave. 'Give us a Kelly, Mister, quick. I got the fiver.'

She rubbed a grubby brown forearm across her wet eyes. Dollars right there in her hand, and still the man stood, steepling his fingers in front of his chest.

It was 1969. Two years earlier there had been a referendum. Vote Yes for Aborigines. Now nobody could stop blacks going where they liked. But this just waltzing in like she owned the place, mind you. No please, no could I. And an axe was a man's business. Nothing good could come of any Abo girl holding an axe.

The woman ignored the wetness rolling down her cheeks. She laid her notes on the counter, smoothed them out. Nothing wrong with them dollars. Nothin' at all. She pressed her palms hard onto the bench.

'Are. You. Deaf?'

'Ah. Thing is. Can't put my hand to one just at the ah. But why not ah come back later, ah. Once you've had a chance to ah.'

The woman snorted. She had had had fifty-one years of coming back later. She pointed through an open doorway to the dozen shining axes tilted against the back wall. On its way to illuminate these gleaming weapons, her index finger silently cursed the man, his formica counter, his cawing hen, his come back later, his ah, his doorway, and every Dugai who had ever stood where she stood, ignorant of the jostling bones beneath their feet.

Her infuriated hiss sent him reeling.

'Sell me one of them good Kellys, or truesgod, Mister, I dunno what I'll do.'

As twenty-year-old Jean got off the bus, she rehearsed her lines. 'I'm strong as strong. Do a man's eight hours in the paddock if need be. Giss a chance, missus.'

When Jean reached the dusty front yard of the farm on Crabbes Creek Road, and saw the swell of May's stomach, hard and round as a melon beneath her faded cotton dress, she knew that she couldn't work here. When May straightened, smiling, from the wash basket, though, and mumbled through the wooden pegs held in her teeth, 'Jean? Oh, thank God you're here,' she thought that perhaps she could.

Ted inched up the driveway that afternoon in a heaving

Holden sedan. Shy and gaunt, he was as reluctant to meet Jean's eye as she was to meet his. This white man would not be turning her door handle at midnight. She decided to stay for a bit. If the baby came out a girl she would just keep going and, anyway, maybe it would be a boy.

The wireless in the kitchen said the Japanese were on the back foot in New Guinea but from Crabbes Creek the war seemed unlikely and very far away. What was real was endless green paddocks stretching to where the scrub began, and after that the ridge of the Border Range, soaring to cleave the Western sky. The hundred-year-old ghost gums along the creek; the lowing of the cows at dawn: these things were real. A tame grey lizard came to breakfast on the veranda, and occasionally Jean would glimpse the wedgetails wheeling far above the mountain, tiny smudges halfway to the sun. May had seen both eagles on the road once, after a loose heifer had got itself killed by the milk truck. You couldn't fathom the hugeness of them, and the magnificent curve of their talons, lancing into the unfortunate Hereford's flank.

Jean fell into a routine of cleaning, cooking, helping May in the garden, and sitting by the wireless at night until Ted began to snore or May said, 'Ah, well.' Of a morning, as she stoked the fire and then went out with an icy steel bucket to milk the bellowing Queenie, Jean would hear May retching and spewing in the thunder box. One day, two months after she first arrived, there was blood on the marital sheets. Jean stripped the bed and ordered May to lie back down on clean linen. Then she took Ted's gun off the wall and shot a young roo from the mob that considered the golden creek flats their own particular kingdom. A life to save another life. Jean made broth from the roo tail. 'And you can just lie there till it's your time,' she said crisply. 'It's not like I can't manage that little patch of weedy nothing you like to call a garden.'

The life inside May fought hard to hang on. Her vomiting eased, and as the weeks passed the terror slowly left her face. When her time drew very near, an obvious question occurred to May: Didn't Jean want children of her own? A husband?

'Not really,' said Jean, 'and who would I marry anyway, and is that Ted home already.'

May ignored the possibility of Ted. 'The war will be over soon, there'll be lots of blokes running about the place. You said you like babies.'

'Yes,' Jean said, expressionless. 'Other people's babies. Now lie flat, or I'll never hear the end of it from Himself.'

'You mean from you.' May laughed, for the doctor had said the danger was past. Baby kicked happily now whenever it heard Ted's voice coming up the stairs.

The next week, Ted drove his wife into Murwillumbah at speed, churning dust and scaring fowl all the way to the hospital. They returned three days later with a squalling bundle on the back seat. Jean held her breath, waiting to discover if she could stay.

'We called him Eric,' Ted told the water tank proudly. 'After me old dad.'

'Eric,' repeated Jean, reaching down to stroke a tiny pink cheek.

Later May reported the doctor's verdict: make the most of this one, because there would be no more babies for her.

★

Eric was a plump laughing baby, and then an adored toddler, always wandering, always in the pots and pans.

'Come to Jean-Jean,' she would cry, and Eric would ball his little fists and hurtle joyfully into her, clutching at her shins. She lifted him high in the air, both of them squealing with delight, until May came out laughing too, and demanded her turn. If the child cried in the night, it didn't matter to him who arrived to comfort him. Eric was at home in the world, because the world had shown him only love and tenderness.

'If it wasn't for the fact that I feed him,' May said casually, tucking herself back into her blouse one day, 'I don't think he'd know that I'm his mother, and not you.'

'Oh, he does!' protested Jean, feeling a sudden thread of fear unspooling in her gut. 'And he's the spit of you, anyway. What would he want with a mother like me?' May glanced at Jean's brown face, her black eyes and matchstick limbs.

'You're not all that dark. You're more like Gina Lollobrigida,' she said generously. 'Exotic. Plenty of men would want you for a wife.'

'But would I want them?' Jean retorted, a question that had never occurred to May.

After that, Jean held the boy a little less when his mother was around. She let May go to him at night, and was careful to be outside more often helping Ted in the paddock when Eric needed his afternoon bath. May thought they were pals, but Jean knew she could be flung away from the farm with one brief word, catapulted back to the Mission, even, if she couldn't scrape a better life up out of her own effort and wits.

★

May confessed tearfully one day that she had briefly allowed Eric – now struggling on her lap to regain his lost freedom – to stray into the Big Paddock. 'I actually felt my heart stop. I never knew you could love anyone so much.'

But I did, thought Jean, with a pang so fierce it made her gasp.

'He's a terror for wandering, alright. Pity we can't bell him like Queenie,' was what she finally managed.

May caught the bus to town and returned with a tinkling ribbon that had six tiny silver bells sewn onto it by kind Mrs O'Connell. With the ribbon pinned between his shoulder blades, Eric could be heard all over the house and yard, a blue cattle bitch lurking by his side as constant as a shadow.

The second time Eric got himself lost, he was gone half an hour. They finally found him playing in the mud on the far side of the duck house, three strides from the dam, the ribbon torn off by the wire around the vegie patch. The women, who had each thought that the other was watching Eric, quietly resolved to say nothing to Ted. That night Jean woke the household screaming that a black snake had got in and bitten the baby – but it was only a bad dream.

It was the barking that alerted them to Eric's third disappearance, a few weeks later. Peeling spuds on the veranda, Jean became aware of the dog's frenzied yelps, and realised that she hadn't heard Eric's bell for a minute or more. She rocketed to her feet, sending spuds all over the silky-oak floorboards, and ran blindly to the yard where the dog was circling in agitation.

Jean and May circumnavigated the house, then the paddocks, with no result. Eric would not be found. A search party fanned out, desperate for clues. Here the boy had scratched at the damp creek bank with a twig from the largest gum. Here he had uprooted one of Queenie's dry pats, to discover what crawling treasures lay beneath. But the signs petered out where the pasture of the Big Paddock turned into scrubby foothills, and nothing was revealed – not that day, nor the next, nor in the awful weeks that followed – that could bring Eric back to them. The boy had quite simply vanished.

Nobody could fathom why Ted and May kept the dark girl on. But who else would understand why Ted could never go straight to the Big Paddock in the mornings anymore, and took the long way past the dam instead? Who else shared May's memory of Eric tilting his head to eat his porridge? The high tinkling bell-note of a king parrot's call made Jean catch May's eye, and neither of them had to say a word. And so the terrible thing that would have driven any other three people far apart, instead bound them together.

In spring, Ted planted a silky oak sapling between the house and the gate. At its foot lay an engraved granite boulder. May took to sitting beside Eric's rock at odd hours of the day and night, gazing past the ghost gums, searching the distant hills. When the wet season arrived they sat, waiting to see what would wash down to them from the forested gullies. But the foaming brown floodwaters of the creek revealed as little as the search parties had. Their vigil, like all of Ted's endless Sunday tramping, scouring the hills, was in vain.

Queenie still lowed at dawn, demanding to be milked. The eagles still wheeled over the ridge. The tame grey lizard still came for crumbs in the morning. Jean ventured out from the house more than before; she learned from Ted how to rope and brand calves, and then to jerkily drive the cattle truck into town. Good as any man with stock, he told her boots. Nobody blamed her; nobody asked her to leave.

Perhaps, Jean reflected wryly, after three more summers had passed, perhaps May *was* a friend, after all.

It was two decades, and a new war in Korea come and gone, before the government letter arrived. *It has been determined by our engineering division.* Ted looked up from the Big Paddock at the hills to be sliced in half by the new highway. May began slamming doors. Soon bulldozers arrived, and men with dynamite. Ted scratched at his scalp. The jungled ridge belonged to the memory of Eric, not to the government. But then what if they turned something up. Hard to know what to think, really.

When the first young protestors came to the door, Ted walked away, but May dried her hands on a tea-towel and listened. 'Don't bother the stock,' she told them, 'and shut them bloody gates.' A village of yurts and Kombis sprang up near the creek. Jean and Ted shook their heads. Girls in muslin dresses staggered up to the house, sunburnt, dehydrated, bitten by spiders. The trees are our brothers, Jean was informed by a boy who needed a lift to hospital the next day, concussed by a falling limb. A jolly fellow with an earring tumbled into the campfire and burned half his face off. At month's end, the remnant kernel of protesters tried, and failed, to scale the largest of the gum trees to stage a sit-in in its canopy.

It wasn't ultimately clear to the district who should bear the blame for the inferno. Most said the protestors, obviously, for lighting campfires in the first place, or May for allowing the city-bred fools on the farm. Some blamed the cop who had deliberately kicked coals towards nylon tents, determined that the hippies be driven out. A few even blamed Ted for failing to maintain his rutted driveway better, so that the fire truck couldn't get to the paddock in time.

After the sirens had faded, and the night was at an end, the firefighters had picked up all their tools and taken them home, and the Kombis had all pulled away from the charred ground in disgrace, Ted, May and Jean slumped on the veranda, filthy and almost too tired for sleep. A profound silence fell upon the farm. No stock remained alive to bellow. The only sounds were the faint shushing of a light breeze through the few pathetic trunks still standing in the blackened smear that was the Big Paddock. That, and a strange high tinkling from beyond the creek.

Bone weary, Jean and May stared at each other. Then they ran, flinging great black clouds of ash in their wake. They forded the creek and ploughed their way through the fire-thinned scrub, until at last they stood below an enormous tallowwood, halfway up the mountain. It was a tree Ted knew; he had eaten a sandwich beneath it more than once on his Sunday treks. The fire had reached it, licked its trunk, caused it to shudder and tremble, but not to fall.

'There.'

Jean pointed up. Ted and May craned their necks, squinting in the first faint streak of dawn light. What tinkled above them was a narrow thread, dislodged from its resting place by the force of the fire, and spinning now in the breeze which blew across the empty paddock. The merest ghost of a belled ribbon, it had been wedged tight in the eagle's nest for thirty years.

Get me an axe, thought Jean.

Forbidden Fruit

Jeanine Leane

Jeanine Leane is a Wiradjuri writer, poet and academic from south-west New South Wales. Her poetry collection, *Dark Secrets After Dreaming: A.D. 1887–1961*, won the Scanlon Prize for Indigenous Poetry; and her first novel, *Purple Threads*, won the David Unaipon Award. Jeanine is the recipient of many awards, including a Red Room Poetry Fellowship, two Australian Research Council Fellowships and the Oodgeroo Noonuccal Prize for Poetry, twice.

It was summer. The air was thick with the syrupy smell of decaying fruit. Lynne stood beneath the apricot trees and felt the tangerine ooze of spent fruit rise through her toes. She had planted the fruit trees years ago when she bought the house with her new husband.

Each year she bottled the fruit. Sealed jars of apricots adorned her pantry shelves long after her marriage ended. They sat marinating in their own juices of captured youth and sweetness untapped.

Lynne prepared to climb the apricot trees and glean this year's harvest. Parting the branches near the fence she came face to face with her new neighbour. He smiled as he gorged himself with fresh fruit: sticky nectar dripping down his forearms. He was scruffy and unkempt – like a hippy, Lynne thought.

Hey, he said. *I hope you don't mind but this fruit is spilling into our backyard.*

Oh … no. Lynne masked her surprise.

Eating fresh fruit is like a religious experience, he continued, oblivious. *So cleansing. I love watching it rot on the ground to become part of next year's richness.*

I usually bottle the fruit, she said curtly, *to save for another day.*

I think that's sad, plucking it at the height of its potential and confining it to jars that may never be opened.

Lynne shrugged.

In the kitchen she prepared to cook the fruit, but the image of arrested youth started haunting her. She stared at the laden shelves: her storeroom of trapped potential.

She abandoned her preserving and sat beneath the fruit trees, inhaling their decadence and contemplating the farcical situation that was her marriage.

Richard had always wanted to save things for another day. She suggested Europe while they were still young and earning good money. He wanted to save.

We can see Europe another time – we don't have to be young, he scoffed.

He was like that when she wanted a baby too. *Let's save our energy,* he said. *The world is overcrowded already with vain people who want to replicate themselves!*

The preserved fruit was his idea and like everything else it was for another day. When he left years later with no Europe and no baby, the bottles of fruit were her only souvenir.

In dreams she felt herself being forced into a jar. Inside the thick glass, apricots became the contorted face of a woman stewing in her own stale juice. Rising, she cleared the pantry shelves. At first light she prised open the lids and began emptying the contents onto the ground.

The hippies from next door gravitated over. *Be free,* they chanted as Lynne scattered years of forbidden fruit onto the garden floor. She was liberated.

She went to Europe. Her neighbours received a postcard from the orchards of Provence.

I'm pregnant! Lynne wrote. *Will be back home in high summer to give birth among the apricots!*

The Golden Wedding Anniversary

Gayle Kennedy

Gayle Kennedy is a Wongaiibon woman of the Ngiyaampaa nation of south-west New South Wales. Her writing has won multiple awards, including the David Unaipon Award for *Me, Antman and Fleabag*, which was also shortlisted for the Victorian Premier's Literary Award and a Deadly Award, and commended for the Kate Challis RAKA Award. Oxford University Press has published eleven of her children's books.

Me, Antman and Fleabag went to Uncle Vic and Aunty Bess's fiftieth wedding anniversary. They're Ant's relations. It was a great party. All Aunty Bess's mob came. Uncle Vic's brother, his wife, kids, their kids and hundreds of their friends. Their only child, Della, came from Brisbane with husband Chris and two children, thirteen-year-old Buddy and ten-year-old Lulu. They had Old Merv Hanrahan as master of ceremonies. Ant reckons he emcees every local event, from christenings to funerals, engagements to weddings, presentations, sporting or otherwise. He got the job years ago cos he owned a suit and was never lost for words. Uncle Vic reckoned Merv had an opinion on everything and everyone, whether you wanted it or not. Also, his wife Dulcie made the best wine trifle in the district and always brought one along, so that didn't hurt either.

The Dandenong Country Drifters were the band for the night. They played country, rock and roll and some waltzes for the older folk, and pretty soon had everyone up dancing. The first one up was Luvvo. Coal black skin, a shock of white hair and the figure of someone twenty years younger, Luvvo could shake it with the best of them. And when she'd throw back her head and yell in her port wine and cigarette growl, 'I still got it,' no one doubted her, least of all the women, young or old. They kept their men folk real close when Luvvo was around.

Later in the evening Bess and Vic danced the Anniversary Waltz. Vic, tall, fair, blue-eyed and sandy-haired. Bess, tiny and dark, with long, thick hair, black but for a few streaks of silver that gave off a sparkle as she danced lightly in his arms. They looked as in love today as they were fifty years ago when they married in the old registry with her mum and dad and his granny looking on.

Then came the speeches. Different ones got up and talked about what a great couple they were. They talked about how they'd turned their property into the best in the district. About their generosity, their terrific family. Della spoke about what fantastic parents they were, how much she and her husband and kids loved and were so proud of them. Vic and Bess was fairly lit up with pride.

Finally Vic got up. He thanked everyone – from his friends, family and the Lord for his wonderful life and the gift of Bess, Della and her family. He and everyone else spoke about everything. Everything but what Della really wanted to hear.

Antman reckoned she'd pestered em for years.

'Please,' she'd beg. 'Tell me how you met. I tell everyone how I met Chris at uni. How we fell in love. How he proposed.'

But they'd just say, 'It doesn't matter.' Or tell her, 'It's in the past. We're together now. That's all that matters.'

She'd ask their friends or relatives but they'd go quiet. Tell her it wasn't up to them to say. Reckoned Vic and Bess would tell her when they were ready. It drove her mad. She'd moan about it to Chris, or me and Ant, and we'd say they probably had their reasons. That just gave her the shits.

After the party, Big Jim West (five foot four in his socks) drove us all home. He'd been the town drunk, proppin up the bar of the Royal Mail from openin to half past drunk for many years. Then he met Ollie who fell in love with the man, not the drunk. Reckoned he was a good sort, just needed sprucin up. She got him sober and he hasn't touched a drop in twenty years. Non-drinkers were a rarity in these parts, and it wasn't long before he became 'designated driver', the town eventually purchasing a community bus of which Big Jim was supreme overlord.

The bus belted along the dirt and gravel moonlit roads. People, full of grog and good cheer, sang out of tune as each family was dropped off in turn, until finally all us mob. We was stayin with Unc and Aunt. Uncle Vic, Chris and Ant went ta bed, they was pretty pissed, so me, Aunty Bess and Della sat out on the wide, screened veranda and sipped cold beer.

'Jeez, Ma, it was a beaut party,' reckoned Della.

'The best thing was you, Chris and the kids comin home,' replied Bess.

'Wouldn't have missed it. Luvvo can still shake it, aye?' said Della, sipping her beer.

'You're not wrong, daught. I told her she better keep her paws off your father, or me and her will be knucklin up.'

'Oh, Ma! Luvvo'd make mincemeat of you.' Della laughed.

Bess chuckled. 'Don't bet on it, bubby. Ya father's worth fightin for.'

We just sat there all quiet, just listenin to the sound of crickets.

Finally Della spoke. 'Ma, please tell me how you met. It can't be that bad.'

'Leave it alone, daught.'

Then the low rumble of Vic's voice disturbed us. We hadn't heard him come out.

'Tell her, Bess. It's about time.'

'Gawd, Vic! Sneakin up like that. You sure?'

'I'm sure. We'll both tell her.'

I said maybe I should go inside and leave em in peace but they reckoned no, I could stay if I wanted.

Vic sat beside Bess and took her tiny, dark hand in his, and after a deep breath, Bess started speaking.

'In those days, men had no respect for us Koori girls. They'd come sneakin round camps at night, bringin grog. Stirrin up trouble. Sometimes they'd chase us home from town. They got one of me cousins. She killed herself not long after. Funny thing though, the day after they did it, they was all down town with their women folk, helpin em with their shoppin, actin right and proper, tippin their hats to all the white ladies. Meanwhile Ruthie's lying bleedin in a hospital bed and no copper would believe her story. Even if they did, they wouldn't have charged em. They were white, we was black, end of story. Who do you reckon the cops believed? After that, men from the camp would go everywhere with us.'

Bess sipped her beer and looked at Vic who squeezed her hand. She took a deep breath and continued.

'Anyway, I had a job in town, cleanin the café. One day me brother was late pickin me up. I got impatient, started walkin home by meself. I was halfway there when I heard the truck. It was drivin slow and I turned around and saw it comin across the paddock. I heard the boys yahooin and laughin. I knew I was in trouble.

'I started runnin so fast I thought me heart was gunna burst. I zigzagged across the paddock, like Ma told me. She reckoned it slowed em down long enough to get away. But it wasn't workin and I tripped over a log and fell down. I thought, I'm gone, they're gunna kill me.

'I heard the truck stop. I heard em yahooin. Then I heard the doors slam. I was prayin to the Lord to get me outta this mess. Promised I would always wait for my brother. Would always do the right thing if he'd save me.

'Then I heard an almighty bang. It was a rifle. I thought they'd kill me right there. They wouldn't just rape me; they'd kill me. Then I thought bugger it, I'm not gunna lay here with me face in the dirt and let em shoot me in the back like a mongrel dog. They was gunna have to look me in the face before they done it. I turned over, and I saw Merv and Big Jim and a couple of other blokes from town. Ya father was standin there with the rifle pointed at em. They was tellin him to calm down. Big Jim was sayin, "She's only a gin. They love it, mate."

'I sat up and looked at em. Then I heard ya father say, "Look at her. She's just a kid. You mob of animals git back in the truck and piss off before I blow ya heads clean off."

'Merv, Jim and the others got back in the truck. Merv was givin ya father cheek. He was sayin he was weak as piss. Accused him of goin soft, of turnin on his mates for an Abo. Ya father told em to piss off. He wasn't muckin round anymore and fired another shot in the air. They got into the truck and took off, still yellin cheek at ya father.

'He walked over to me and, somehow, I just knew it was gunna be okay.'

Della's face was white. Tears were streaming down her face. Even if she had wanted to speak, she wouldn't have been able to. She was struck dumb by what she was hearing. Vic continued the story.

'Gawd I felt like a bastard. Stupid too. The lads asked me to go huntin. I thought they meant for wild pigs or roos. When they saw Bess walkin and started yelling, "There's one, let's git her," I couldn't believe it. I was tellin em to wake up to their selves. But they wouldn't take any notice.

'Big Jim kept drivin like a maniac. Then Bessie fell and Jim stopped the truck. They jumped out and I knew what they were gunna do. I couldn't let it happen so I grabbed me rifle and fired it into the air. They were full of cheek, but like the cowards they were, they weren't gunna take the chance so they left. I walked over to ya mother. She looked so little and helpless, but she seemed to trust me so that when I put the gun down and offered her me hand, she took it and I helped her stand up. She was shakin and terrified. Then I looked into the brownest eyes I've ever seen. I knew there and then I'd marry her. No matter what, Bess was gunna be my wife.

'While we were standin there a mob arrived from her camp. They were in a panic. They thought someone had been shot. They saw me and ya mother. Saw the shotgun on the ground. I explained what had happened. Told em how sorry I was. How ashamed I was. Bess's dad asked me back to the camp for a cuppa. Told me I was a bigger man than those mongrels would ever be.

'Then I started goin back all the time. Just to visit Bess.

I remember the first day I drove her and me to the pictures. Everyone was lookin at us. In those days they made Aboriginal people sit in a roped-off section of the theatre. So I sat with her there.'

Bessie squeezed his hand and continued on with the story.

'The manager came up and told him that he shouldn't sit there. It was for the Abos. He said he was with me and if I couldn't sit in the other section then he wasn't gunna either. Gawd we copped some shit. We'd walk up the street and blokes would call him a gin jockey. He wanted to belt em, but I wouldn't let him. He'd just wind up in gaol. They weren't worth it.

'Then he asked me to marry him. I told him he was off his rocker. I didn't mind if he just came and visited me, took me out. But I told him he'd be better off marrying a white girl. I told him his family would hit the roof. He said he didn't care.'

'And she was right, baby girl,' said Vic. 'I didn't care. She was then, and she still is, the only girl for me.

'I asked her father for her hand, he said yes, but he warned us of the hard road ahead. I took her home and me folks hit the roof. Said they'd cut me outta the will. I'd git nothin. But me old grandma said me and Bess could have her old property. She reckoned we could make a go of it. She loved Bess from the day she met her. And we did make a go of it. Together we made it the best sheep station around. Then you come along and, well, everything's been great.'

Della looked at them. 'How could you forgive Old Merv and Big Jim? How could you speak to those animals let alone be their friends? There was Merv talking at the party about what a wonderful couple you are. How great Mum is. He's nothing but a fucking hypocrite.'

Bess took Della's hand and quietly said, 'Darlin, I didn' bring you up to use language like that.'

'What do you mean language like that?' screamed Della. 'Those men are pigs!'

Vic stood up and walked over to the edge of the veranda and, after what seemed an eternity, said, 'I don't expect you to understand, but when we got married something came over Merv. He came over one day with Dulcie. She had a trifle with her. Ya ma asked em in and Merv stood there with his hat in his hand and he asked for our forgiveness. Said it had been preyin on his mind. Dulcie reckoned he'd been evil, but he should say sorry and ask for forgiveness and even if we refused, at least he'd tried to be a decent man and make up for what he done.

'I said it was up to ya ma. She was cryin and said of course she'd forgive him. We cracked a couple of bottles of beer and we've been friends ever since. Through thick and thin. Hatred gets ya nowhere, bubby. I thought we'd taught you that.

'Big Jim felt bad too. But he took to the drink until he got married. Even then it took a few years for him to say he was sorry. They were the only two that did. None of the other boys did. But we didn't and we still don't need em in our lives, bubby.'

Bess stood up and taking Vic's hand said, 'It's time we was goin to bed. You need time to think things through, bub. Just remember, me and ya father had the best marriage. We wouldn't change a thing. A lot of women never find the measure of their men. I saw his the minute I met him. It doesn't matter how we met. What matters is that we met.'

Della sat in the dark for a long time after. I sat there with her, just holdin her hand. Hot, salty tears were soaking her face and dampening the crisp, white cotton of her party dress. She couldn't get over what had happened and kept askin why.

She felt angry that her beautiful mother had gone through such brutality. And, worse, it had been at the hands of men she had known and trusted all her life. She asked me how she could look at them in the same way anymore. I reckoned I didn't know.

Then she felt a strong hand on her shoulder and looked up at the sad face of her husband.

'You heard?' she asked.

'Yeh. Let it go, Dell. It was their decision to forgive. It's nothing to do with you.'

Della told me the next day that she wanted to scream at him. Ask him if he could understand how she felt. But in her heart she knew that he was right. Anger was their prerogative, not hers. She wiped the tears from her eyes with the hem of her dress, took his hand and said, 'Let's go to bed. It's been a long night.'

I reckoned it had.

Born, Still

Jane Harrison

Playwright and author **Jane Harrison** is descended from the Muruwari people. Her plays include *Stolen*, *Rainbow's End* and *The Visitors*. Her novel *Becoming Kirrali Lewis* won the 2014 black&write! Writing Fellowship, and was shortlisted for the Prime Minister's Literary Awards and the Victorian Premier's Literary Awards.

Friday afternoon. The colour of the sky. The yellow green of jacaranda leaves against the intense blue sky.

It is August. I sit on the edge of the hospital bed, looking out the window. There is nothing else to do. Yellow green against blue.

It's midafternoon. I wait alone.

Yesterday, Thursday, and I am wiping the kitchen cupboards. The brand-new kitchen is covered in fine brown building dust. It's warm for August, which is why Possum is running around wearing only a T-shirt. Wipe, wipe, rinse the cloth. Then I am lying down on the cheap sofa we'd installed while we owner-built. An island of foamy comfort in the tsunami of a building site.

'Mummy, why are you lying down?'

My two-and-a-half-year-old, who seldom saw me prone. Especially with a house to build. Especially as a mother of a two-and-a-half-year-old.

'Mummy's waiting to feel the baby move.'

I am thirty-six weeks pregnant. Hugely. Since it's my second baby I don't look like I have a size-five basketball shoved up my T-shirt – it's more like a big messy pillow.

'Is the baby moving?'

'Not yet.'

'Why?'

'I'm not sure. Let's just lie still together and see.'

I lie still. There's so many jobs still to do. Small tedious jobs, like wiping cupboards, and big jobs, like packing up the rented house, painting walls and building steps to the veranda. Who would owner-build? It's never finished. Never finished until you split up and have to sell it and then it's finished and fabulous. But never before then.

Possum has wriggled off, out of sight. I hear her grunt, at the same time I hear a car on the gravel driveway. The latter is the TV antenna man, winding his way up the long drive. The grunt is that of the toddler who has taken a dump on the lounge-room floor. Shit! Literally.

'Just a minute!' I call out to the antenna man. Where's the paper towel?

Friday morning. I am wearing my mother-in-law's coat, bought in London when she was thirty. She knows I like old things. It's not 'vintage couture' but it serves its purpose. Can't tell if I am fat, or pregnant, or pregnant and fat.

I am shopping with my sister-in-law. I need slippers. I should have been more organised.

In the lead-up my mother said, 'Do you have your port ready?' Who calls them 'ports' these days? No, my port is not packed. I am not organised. Now if I had some help ...

I did ask. My mother said, 'When do I have time to help?' She is too busy being retired, painting pictures and maintaining the garden (it's a big job). But still.

Pissed off, I ring my sister. She is always happy to trade

complaints about our mother. But she's in one of those moods. I do my 'poor me' routine; her eyes narrow. I know, it's a phone call, but I can feel her eyes narrowing down the phone line. I step into the trap. 'Can you come and help me?' I whine.

'When did you ever help me? When I was pregnant and we were moving into our new house, surrounded by mud. When did you give me a hand?' She goes on and on. That was twenty-one years ago! I was sixteen. I didn't have a driver's licence. There was no public transport to where she lived; I was doing my HSC and as useful as a chocolate teapot.

Did I say any of this to her? No. I listened and then I got off the phone and sobbed. And not for, like, three hours. Literally three hours. And I vowed, I am never going to speak to either of them, ever again. Not even if something really bad happens. I am never going to speak to them again.

Something bad happens.

Friday arvo. I sit on the tightly made hospital bed staring at the jacaranda leaves. I have a newspaper for company, bought from the booth in the hospital foyer. My sister-in-law has left. I urged her to go; she has a long drive home.

I have been induced with prostaglandin gel. It will be hours before my husband arrives as he is moving house. Flicking through the arts section of the paper, I see my old friend Greg has won a short film award. Yeah, go Greg, awesome. I want to ring and congratulate him, but I don't have his number. Also, it might be awkward to talk to him right now.

God, I really should ring my mother.

Thursday afternoon. The antenna man has left. The poo has been cleaned up. Possum has a nappy on. I lie on the couch. We brought up a few pieces of furniture, because, as owner-builders, we were here so much. A kettle, a table, folding chairs, the couch. I lie waiting for the baby to wriggle, to dance the merengue. Waiting.

Finally, I ring my obstetrician. I can't feel the baby move. He tells me to come into the hospital.

'Have I got time to shower?'

I am grimy from the kitchen cupboards. I have been living in these trackie daks for weeks. The same trackie daks. You only have one pair, when you are pregnant. A humungous pair.

'Yes, have a shower, then come in.'

Have I got time for Nick to come home from work so we can drive up together?

'Yes, come in together.'

He sounds calm. I call Nick and he leaves work, a little earlier than usual, but that's okay, he's the boss. The three of us pile in the car. In the country everything is sixty kilometres away. I've had my shower and I've thrown a few things together, just in case. But I haven't packed my 'port'.

'Sorry you had to leave work early,' I apologise to Nick. He's okay about it.

At the hospital we are ushered into the ultrasound area. The midwife is upbeat as she smears my belly with the gel, cold and oozy, thick and clammy. She swipes the instrument across and across and across my broad belly. She remains cheerful. She leaves to fetch another midwife. The second midwife repeats the motions of the first.

'Sometimes the heartbeat is obscured by other body parts,' the second midwife says, also cheerful.

'Let me know when I should start crying,' I say, because I'm not one for hysteria, because I'm not going to be one of those neurotic types of pregnant women, am I? But they don't reply, they don't reassure me. They continue to smile but leave to ring the doctor. We wait. It's probably his dinner time.

The obstetrician hasn't ever met my husband but doesn't introduce himself or hold out his hand for a handshake. He gets straight down to it.

'I am afraid the worst has happened.'

Does he always say that? Did he rehearse that line on the way in?

I don't cry yet. He tells me that I can continue to carry the baby until I go into labour naturally – there's no hurry – or I can be induced. I book in to be induced the next day.

I am carrying a dead thing. Where there was life and hope and dreams and a future human with a name already chosen, there is now death. Inside me. I scream, 'Get it out of me.' But I'm just *thinking* the scream, I don't actually do it. But I do cry. I am human.

We leave the hospital and by now it's seven thirty and two-and-a-half-year-olds need food, no matter the emotional devastation and the fact that Mummy is weeping. Naturally we go to McDonald's, conveniently situated on the freeway out of town. I'm red-eyed but holding it together. Ordering normally. Waiting for our order normally.

The young McDonald's girl hands over the food. 'Have a nice night,' she says. Normally.

'What the fuck, my baby has just died. How can I have a good night?' I don't yell at her, because she is fifteen or sixteen , and why ruin her night too? Imagine how traumatised she would be, poor thing.

The country shack we are renting while we build the 'dream home' has gently undulating floors and is held together with pink priming paint. The landlords are salt of the earth but the house should be razed. I decide that I can't come home from hospital to this dump. So we agree to move as planned, the next day, Friday, to our half-built house on the hillside.

There is a knock at the door. Unexpectedly, it is my brother and sister-in-law, on their way home from a camping holiday. They thought they'd pop in to say hello. Hello! They are greeted at the door by our swollen-eyed faces. They offer to stay the night. My sister-in-law will drive me to the hospital in the morning while David helps Nick with the move.

Friday morning. I shuffle past the removalists, wearing the heavy coat that obscures my belly, my head down, sobbing. I wonder if anyone tells them why. At least it is a good excuse for how disorganised we are. On the way, we stop to buy slippers. I dread anyone asking me when I am due. I avoid people's eyes. At the counter of the department store I pick up a bulk pack of man-sized hankies.

It's Friday afternoon. I have read the paper. I have not rung Greg, the award-winning director.

I stare at the jacaranda. I ring my mother from the hospital payphone. It is her grandchild after all, and she needs to hear it from me.

The world doesn't shift on its axis.

Friday evening. I think I ate the hospital food. Nick has arrived, exhausted. The doctor has given me another application of gel. I haven't dilated. The hospital is quiet, all the visitors gone. We have the whole place to ourselves. We sprawl in the waiting area and share a bottle of red wine. It's not going to make much difference now, is it?

As my family are hours away, Possum is staying at her family day carer's. It is her first night away from us, ever. Later, Pauline gives me a photo of her in the bath, a polaroid. She doesn't look distressed. She looks … inscrutable.

Tuesday before. My regular visit to the obstetrician. I am thirty-five weeks pregnant and will be induced in two weeks, given my gestational diabetes.

He is listening to the heartbeat and I have this urge to ask him if I can listen too, but he only has a stupid old-fashioned cone, like a mini megaphone. Then, as I am walking out, he casually asks me if I've been having many movements lately. 'Not as many as with Possum,' I reply. Now *she* was a kickboxer. Once I saw the outline of her foot through my skin, like it was poking through Glad Wrap.

That casually asked question while I was already heading out the door. I think about it later, with the benefit of hindsight. But then? I did not have any inkling that anything was wrong, except for that urge to listen to the heartbeat. Some mother's intuition. While he must have known and was waiting for me to discover it for myself. That's why he told me to take my time.

The previous Wednesday day, in bed. Completely wrecked. I had been varnishing the timber edge of the kitchen benchtop. Anyone who's ever been pregnant knows that when you are still, that's when the baby kicks. It's not kicking. My husband, who has never been pregnant, says, 'Things often go quiet just before the birth.' Humph. That's when I started to get anxious.

Saturday morning. Four am. I am on my hands and knees. The contractions are strong and regular. I am fully dilated. The doctor is summoned. I feel for him, being called in at this hour on a Saturday to deliver a dead baby.

I have gas for the pain. I didn't have anything for Possum's birth, my all-natural woohoo birth. Now, it's not even significant that I have gas.

It's quick and silent. There are no reassuring words. No: 'You're doing really well'; 'It won't be long now.' Silence.

I gasp in the gas. I am doing really well.

There's a complication. I don't know what the doctor is doing but it hurts. I hurt in silence. Sucking that gas. Maybe that's what they mean by 'suck it up'.

It's done. There is no newborn baby cry, the most reassuring sound in the world.

Silence.

'What did I have?'

'A girl. We had a girl.'

Like, why did I have to ask? Doesn't anyone think it matters? We only had one named picked, a girl's.

They show her to me, wrapped up in a bunny rug. Luckily I'm not squeamish. Her skin has peeled – it is explained to me – because she has been dead for a while. Making me wonder when I had last felt her kick or move. How shocking, how negligent of me, not to notice that. What with the owner-building, the toddler, the finishing up at work … Poor little thing.

Actually, she's not so little. She's a boofer. Eight pound eight, with broad shoulders. That was the complication. He had to reach in, to break her little shoulder to get her out. Another indignity.

She looks like me. Poor thing. Boofy, peeled face.

The staff at the hospital are great. They hang a butterfly symbol on the door of our private room. It lets the staff know there has been a stillborn or SIDS baby, so that people don't say anything inappropriate, or act cheerful around us like we have just produced a miracle. They take polaroids of her, wrapped in her bunny rug. They give us a small booklet containing a tuft of her strawberry blonde hair, her foot and handprints, her weight and date of birth.

We are told to take our time.

Her sister is brought in, with the paternal grandparents. Possum holds the baby and another Polaroid is taken, this time Possum's face is clouded. Do you think that's cruel, subjecting her to death? She is more comfortable with the experience, I think, than my in-laws, who don't really feel too comfortable hanging out with a dead baby, being of the 'sweep-it-under-the-carpet' era. Still, they are here to support us.

It is now midafternoon and even though we have been told to take our time, we feel we should vacate the room. Possum says goodbye to her baby sister. We leave the baby, swaddled in the yellow bunny rug. We have the little booklet and the Polaroids.

We wind up the long driveway to our semi-finished home and there is a glorious sunset, the full blood-orange and tequila version, to welcome us home. It really is a heavenly spot.

The house: there are boxes everywhere and the electrician is still working, even though it is sunset on a Saturday.

'Sorry,' he says, about the baby, not the lack of electricity. He is the father of five. The power isn't going on tonight but it doesn't matter.

We potter about, putting things in place. The in-laws stay

two days and then, seeing we can 'cope', they leave. The power is finally connected.

Flower arrangements begin to arrive, and visitors with gifts, mainly plants. My sister and mother arrive. I have made a nice lunch for them. Amazing that one can do stuff like that, on automatic pilot.

Like a time-lapse photo of a fungus growing in a petri dish, the flower arrangements multiply. It's a high tide of flowers and the cards are like driftwood. We decide not to have a funeral, but have a gathering and my friend Bek plays the flute while a big mob of us plant trees for a forest in her memory.

The Tuesday after. I smell like a dim-sim factory. I have cabbage leaves in my bra. Old wives' tale, supposedly helps with the discomfort. My boobs don't know that the baby died. My milk has come in and it's friggin' painful. My breasts are engorged, rock hard, and I'm weepy. Every few hours I change the cabbage leaves for fresh ones. Maybe it's just the cold of the leaves but it is a relief.

People say, 'I don't know what to say.' That's okay. What's not okay is 'bummer'. True – that's how one friend responded when I told him my baby had died. 'Bummer' is when your footy team loses the semi by a point. 'Bummer' is when the scoop falls off your ice-cream cone three licks in. Please don't say, 'It's nature's way.' Or, 'It was probably for the best.' You don't know that. People cross the road to avoid me. When I go back to work, still numb, the childless librarian says, 'I expect you want to take your mind off it.' No, I don't want to take my mind off 'it'. You do. You don't want my sadness to remind you that a tragic thing happened. It's like I'm somehow diseased, contagious. Then there's the nurturers. Who fuss. Who prepare casseroles. Actually I didn't get too many of them. Maybe I'm too too too too stoic.

It's six months later. For an old bird, I do okay. Bang, so to speak, and I'm pregnant again. I'm not too anxious. I'm not fearful. I don't think 'it' is gunna happen again. But the baby is precious. They all are, but this one is precious.

I'm driving down the hill with Possum, now three and a bit. She still wants her baby sister. She asks, 'Is this baby going to be happy?' I reassure her. This baby is going to be happy. And she is.

Frank Slim

Tony Birch

Tony Birch is the author of three novels – *The White Girl*, *Ghost River* and *Blood* – and four short story collections. He has been shortlisted for the Miles Franklin twice, and has won the NSW Premier's Award for Indigenous Writing and the Victorian Premier's Literary Award for Indigenous Writing. In 2017 he was awarded the Patrick White Literary Award for his contribution to Australian literature. In 2021 he will release a poetry book and a short story collection with UQP.

Viola fell for the boy at first sight, leaving her no choice but to care for him. Her brothel was orderly and maintained rules, and near the top of the list was that her girls couldn't bring their kids into work. It was a decision governed by common sense. Viola had a solid relationship with the local police, one that didn't come cheap. Every copper at the station, from senior detectives to young recruits on the beat, put a hand out to look the other way. Social Welfare was a different story entirely. They couldn't be accommodated with either sex or money. Any evidence that a minor had frequented a brothel and the business would be threatened with closure. So, when Else Booth turned up at work one afternoon with a ten-year-old boy, Viola was ready to read the riot act to her. Else raised a hand in her defence.

'I know the rules, Vee, no kids. I only need to leave him for a couple of hours. There's an emergency I have to deal with tonight.'

'Like what emergency?' Viola asked, suspiciously. 'You're paid well here, Else. You have no excuse for working off the books.'

'It's nothing like that. This morning I got a call from one

of my mum's neighbours. Mum's had a fall and has been taken to hospital. They're keeping her in and I need to visit. Take in some soaps and a nightie for her.'

The boy stood in the doorway, staring at the wooden floor, listening to every word. He was slightly built, delicate even, and wore his dark hair long. The child could easily be mistaken for a girl.

'How bad is she, your mother?' Viola asked.

'I won't know until I see her.'

The house cat, Easy, wandered into the kitchen, looked up at the boy and nestled at his feet. He kneeled and petted the cat.

'Okay, you go then,' Viola said, 'but be back here by five o'clock to pick him up. I can't have him around when the show kicks off.'

Else said, 'Thanks, Vee,' and kissed Viola on the cheek. She walked over to the boy and asked him to stand up. She lifted his chin and whispered, 'I'll see you soon,' before hugging him and leaving the house by the back gate. Soon after, Viola heard a car exit the laneway in a hurry. A woman driven by experience and intuition, Viola knew in that moment that Else would not be back at five o'clock, or anytime soon.

Viola turned to the boy. 'What do they call you, love?'

He raised his head and said, 'Gabriel', in a whisper.

Viola had not seen a more beautiful child. His cheeks were flushed rouge, he had long eyelashes and his deep brown eyes, seeped with sadness, reinforced a sense of innocence. Viola, a hard woman at the best of times, could not avoid touching him. She ran the back of her hand across his cheek and through his hair. 'You must be hungry. Sit down and I'll make you a sandwich and a cup of tea.'

As the girls shuffled in for the evening shift, they were equally taken with the boy. More than one of them referred to him as a little angel, without knowing his name. That night he slept in Viola's room, on the chaise longue in the bay window, beneath an expensive Persian blanket that one of her regular customers had given her as a gift. Although she hadn't worked the floor for years, many of Viola's favourites continued to visit. She would pour them a drink, sit and reminisce about the old days before sending the men upstairs with one of her girls, thirty years younger than the client, at a minimum.

Gabriel sat and quietly ate breakfast at the table the following morning. The boy didn't ask about his mother, not that day, the day after, or in the weeks that followed. Else's name was rarely mentioned and no explanation for her disappearance was asked for or offered. Viola suspected that one of Else's regulars had fallen for her and promised her something more than working nights in a brothel. Other girls had been swept off their feet in the same manner, but such arrangements rarely included taking on responsibility for a child and were generally doomed to failure. Sometimes the proposed elopement was a ruse; the new boyfriend secretly intent on putting his lover to work. A pimp took a bigger slice of earnings than a brothel madame, was about as reliable as a cheap watch and easily roused to use his fists.

Sitting across from the boy that morning, Viola realised she was about to break her own cardinal rule. Later that day she sent the house manager, Johnny Circio, out to buy a single bed and set it up in her room. Viola also handed Johnny a roll of notes. He was to take Gabriel into a department store in the city and get him a new wardrobe and a haircut.

'Why this kid?' Johnny asked, after returning to the house with shopping bags full of new clothes, shoes and underwear for the boy. 'I thought you don't like kids?'

'Maybe I feel sorry for him?' she answered, casually, attempting to hide an immediate and deep affection for the boy she could hardly explain to herself.

Johnny laughed. 'Come on, Viola. You've never felt sorry for anyone in your life.'

She didn't like being challenged and put him in his place. 'Mind your business, Johnny. I pay you to keep this house in order, not interrogate me. If you feel a need to behave like a copper, go get yourself a sheriff's badge and a bad haircut.'

'Take it easy, Vee. I'm only asking. He seems like a sweet kid.'

Viola stood at the bay window, parted the velvet curtain and looked out to the street. 'He is sweet. I don't know how, growing up around Else. I've had more than fifty girls come through here and none of them have been as wild as her. He looks as innocent as a doe, and I want it to stay that way. Be sure he doesn't go upstairs and keep him away from the side door, so he's not running into customers. Or police coming by for the collect.'

'So, I'm supposed to be a babysitter now?'

'You're what I pay you to be. I don't want the dirt of this place rubbing off on him. By the way, I need you to get him into school. You can put him down the road with the nuns. Use your home address.'

'The nuns? What if they find out he's living here with you? They'll kick him out.'

'No, they won't. They'd only work harder on saving him.

If we send him to one of the state schools and they find out he's here, the head teacher will be on the phone to Welfare in a blink and he'll be put straight in a Home. One quality I've always admired in the Micks; they never give up on a wayward soul. They'd have persevered with Hitler.'

Viola enjoyed having the house to herself after breakfast time. The girls were gone by seven in the morning and the house was cleaned and empty by nine. She'd make herself a pot of tea and send Johnny off with the laundry and a shopping list, leaving her to sip her tea and read the newspaper. Johnny had enrolled Gabriel at the local Catholic school and, while the boy was not overly familiar with learning, he seemed to enjoy the new experience of having a regular routine.

One morning, soon after Viola had kissed Gabriel on the cheek and sent him off to school, she noticed his lunchbox on the kitchen table. A few minutes later she heard a noise at the side door and assumed he was returning home to fetch it. She got up from the table, walked into the hallway and looked across at the brass knob on the door. She watched as it was turned one way and then the other, followed by a loud knock.

Viola opened the door. 'Gabriel, what are you ...'

She looked into the dark eyes of Des Mahoney. He was a small-time criminal with a reputation for thieving from street prostitutes and backyard bookies, people with no place to turn when they'd been robbed. Mahoney hadn't done any prison time, a clear indication that the man was also a police informant; any decent criminal avoided him. There were also rumours he had an attraction to younger girls. The stories alone were enough for Viola to despise him.

'What do you want at my door?' Viola asked, displaying as much hostility as she could muster. 'We're shut.'

Mahoney closed one eye and fixed on her with the other. 'I was looking for one of your girls, Else Booth. She owes me money.'

'Too bad. She hasn't been here for weeks.'

'When's she due back?'

Viola noticed that Des had stuck a foot in the doorway. She rested an open hand on the back of the door, in case she needed to slam it in his face. 'She won't be back. Else has moved on.'

He shook his head, feigning disgust. 'That's no good to me. I got hold of some perfumes for her. French gear. She hasn't paid me for 'em.'

As far as Viola was concerned the perfume story stunk.

'You've waited some time to collect, Des. Like I said, she's not coming back. You'll have to track her down yourself.' She tried to close the door, jamming his boot.

'I need the money,' he snarled.

'I don't have time for this. I'm busy.' She pushed her shoulder against the door, shutting it in his face.

Viola went into her bedroom and opened the curtains on the sunny morning, feeling a little anxious about Des Mahoney. It wasn't uncommon for a customer to knock at the brothel door after hours, and sending them on their way caused no drama. But Mahoney had unnerved her in a way Viola was not used to. She decided to calm herself by running a bath and was about to take off her dressing-gown when she heard a creaking floorboard in the hallway.

Des Mahoney pushed the door open. He was holding a knife in his hand and smiling at Viola, a mouthful of rotting teeth on display. Viola studied the knife. The blade was short, maybe only three inches long, but well sharpened, by the look of it. Without a weapon in his hand, she wouldn't have hesitated to take Mahoney on. Viola had battled many men over the years, and had the scars to show for her losses and occasional victories, but she wasn't about to risk her neck.

'You can't be coming in here. I'll call my manager, Johnny. He won't put up with this.'

'We both know your errand boy's not here. I seen him leave earlier.' Des waved the knife in the air. 'I want what I'm fucken owed.'

Viola remained calm. 'All right, then. How much is it? Let me settle for Else.'

'I'll take whatever the house is holding, and' – he lunged at her with the knife, nicking Viola on the cheek, just below an eye – 'I'll take whatever else I fancy.'

Gabriel had left the schoolyard immediately after first bell. He ran through the streets to Viola's and picked up his lunchbox from the kitchen table. He was about to leave the house when he heard a shout from one of the front rooms. He walked through the kitchen, along the hallway, and stopped at Viola's bedroom door, hesitating before opening it. When he did, he saw Viola on her bed, lying on her stomach, with her face turned to the wall. Her dressing-gown was hitched up around her shoulders, exposing her naked body. He saw a man standing by the bed with a knife in his hand. Gabriel turned to run and fell. The man leaped across the room and grabbed him by the neck before he could get to his feet. Gabriel was thrown across the room and slammed against the side of the bed. Mahoney bent forward to be sure Gabriel got a look at his knife.

'And who are you, darling?' he asked, in an almost gentle voice.

Gabriel was too terrified to speak.

Mahoney used the blade to lift Gabriel's fringe from his face. He whistled, a low catcall, and rested a hand on Gabriel's thigh, lightly massaging it.

'Hey,' he said, quietly. 'Don't you be frightened, gorgeous. Viola and I are just talking.'

Gabriel had no idea what the man wanted but knew that Viola was in trouble. He began to cry and squeezed his eyes together.

Mahoney tapped the boy on the chin to get his attention. 'I'm not here to hurt anyone, not today.' He reached across the bed to where Viola lay, patted her on the hip and drew her dressing gown down. He picked up a diamond bracelet sitting on the bedside table and held it to the light. 'This will have to do for what Else owes me.'

He put the bracelet in his pocket, looking over at Gabriel. 'Hey, Viola. I'm coming back next week. Same time. You have one of your girls stay back for me. Unless you're willing to step up yourself.' He tousled Gabriel's hair. 'What a lovely looking thing. You do the right thing by me, Viola – if not I'll have to get in touch with the old Welfare molls. They'll fucking treasure this kid.' He slowly stroked Gabriel's head. 'Either them or someone else will.'

The boy listened to the man's heavy footsteps walking

back along the hallway. He waited until he heard the side door close and jumped onto Viola's bed. She reached out to him and started rocking him gently in her arms, kissing him on the forehead. She wiped the blood from her face and looked up at the ceiling.

When Viola heard Johnny return to the house she called him into her room. It had taken her precious little time to realise what she had to do. Gabriel lay in her bed, sleeping peacefully. Johnny could see the bruise across one eye and the fine cut below the other.

'Fuck! What's happened to you, Vee.'

'Nothing I'm about to talk to you about.'

'You will so,' he protested. 'Someone's hurt you. Who the fuck done this?'

Viola took Johnny's hand in hers, the only show of affection she'd provided him in twenty-five years. 'Listen, Johnny. There's something important I need you to do. You can't afford to get it wrong.' She squeezed his hand. 'So, will you listen? Please?'

Johnny wasn't able to listen. He was full of rage. 'Fuck this. You've been given a belt and I need to know who by.'

She gripped his hand. 'Shut up!' She pointed to her bruised eye. 'Do you reckon somebody would do this to me if they thought I had a hard man running the house with me? It's not what you do, Johnny, and never has been.'

Johnny dropped his head in shame.

She squeezed his hand a second time. 'Hey, it's not your fault. I never employed you to be a heavy. You're better than that. Police are supposed to look after me. I pay them enough, but they've grown fat and lazy on handouts. I need to be able to rely on you. Can I do that?'

'Yes, Vee. Of course you can.'

She reached into her dressing-gown pocket and handed Johnny an envelope.

'There's more than enough cash there. Book a hotel room in the city for me. A couple of nights should be enough. The Australia Hotel. There's no sticky noses or riffraff. Then I want you to organise for my stuff – clothes, perfumes, anything personal – to be packed up in boxes.'

Gabriel sighed and rolled from his side onto his stomach. Viola went over to the bed and sat with him.

'The boy's things as well.'

'And what will I do with them?' Johnny asked.

'Telephone Bobby Featherstone, the removalist, and pay him to move the boxes. Have him hold them until I've resettled me and the boy. I'll be in touch with you when the time comes to deliver everything.'

'Resettled? Are you going somewhere?'

Viola ignored the question and handed Johnny a bunch of keys. 'These are for the doors, the money safe and the liquor cabinet.'

'What am I supposed to do with them?'

'Whatever you like. The house is yours, starting tomorrow. You can run it however you want to.'

'I can't run this place on my own.'

'Of course you can. You've been here long enough, you know the business as well as I do. Even better than me when it comes to organisation. Besides, the girls love you, Johnny. You've never once laid a finger on any of them the whole time you've worked here. They trust you.'

'But what about you? You're running away from someone. I know it. I can't believe you'd do that.'

Viola sat back. She felt beaten and worn out. 'Don't you be judging me. I've had enough. I'm too old to take on another battle.'

Gabriel moaned.

Viola moved across the bed, held his body to hers and cradled him until the boy settled. 'I need you to get him out of here tonight. Can you take him to your place until tomorrow morning and I'll come by and pick him up?'

'Sure. The wife will fall in love with him.'

'Good. And there's one last thing I need you to do.'

'Whatever you ask, Vee.'

'You find Frank Slim for me. Tell him I have a job that needs doing in a hurry.'

Around midnight Viola walked through the backyard of a dingy boarding house and into the kitchen. An elderly man sat at a table reading a foreign-language newspaper. Viola recognised his face, having occasionally seen the man coming out of one of the local gambling clubs.

'Des Mahoney?' she asked. 'We need his room. Now.'

The man pointed above his head. 'Is here.'

She climbed the stairs, walked to the door at the end of the landing and turned to the man accompanying her. She nodded. He stepped in front of her and opened the door. The room stunk of cigarette smoke and piss. A kerosene lamp was burning on a table under a window, and empty beer bottles lined the mantle above a blocked fireplace. One wall of the room was covered with pictures of naked women. They'd been torn from magazines. Another wall was papered with clothing-catalogue images of girls, some teenagers, others much younger. Mahoney lay asleep on his bed, nursing an empty bottle. He was covered with a grubby sheet.

Viola walked over to the bed and shook him. 'It's wake-up time, Desmond.'

He didn't move. She shook him more vigorously, stepped back and waited. Mahoney slowly opened one eye, then the other, and looked up. 'What the fuck?'

'I've come to introduce you to somebody, Des.'

Frank Slim stepped out of Viola's shadow. He wore a black suit and tie and sported a crew cut. His dark skin was lined with fine wrinkles, uncommon for a man who never seemed to worry. Des sat up. He was naked. Mahoney knew without having to ask that the man standing alongside Viola could only be Frank Slim. He swallowed the lump in his throat.

'What do you want, Viola?' His voice quivered.

She answered by giving the slightest nod to Slim. He stepped forward and smashed Mahoney in the mouth with a closed fist, knocking his front teeth into his throat. A second punch broke his nose. Slim dragged Mahoney from the bed, knocked him to the floor and systematically kicked him on both sides of his rib cage, his back, arms and legs. Mahoney collapsed in front of the fireplace. Slim buried the heel of a boot into Mahoney's collarbone, dislocating it. Mahoney spat a mouthful of blood and several teeth onto the floor.

Viola raised a hand in the air and Slim stood back. She picked up the kerosene lamp. Mahoney's nose had shifted across his face. He looked up at Viola, spitting more blood.

'You fucking bitch. Cunts like you always need a man to do your dirty work.'

'I thought you were an ignorant bastard, Des. But you're so right. I do need a man.' Viola winked. 'What would you have a woman do after you've beaten her? Call the police? You know what I think, Des? If I were to get in touch with the coppers and tell them what you did to me, it might cost you as much as a round of drinks and a couple of cartons of cigarettes for them to forget the whole thing. Well, you can fuck that. What's happening right now in this shithole is my dirty work, delivered by my hired help. And guess what, Des? I wonder if you know who will be paying? I'll give you a clue. It won't be me.'

'Get fucked, slut.'

Frank Slim waited for Viola to lower her hand. He moved quickly. Neither Mahoney nor Viola saw the flick-knife emerge from the sleeve of his suit pocket and slice a piece out of Mahoney's left ear. Before Des could scream out in pain, Slim swung a leg back and kicked Mahoney between the legs, expelling the air from his body. He gasped as the pain shot into his throat. Mahoney vomited, pissed himself and passed out.

Viola turned to Frank Slim. 'Wait downstairs.' She sat down on a rickety wooden chair until Mahoney came to.

When he eventually sat up his face was unrecognisable. Blood ran from his ear, down the side of his neck and onto his chest.

Viola spoke calmly. 'You're not to go near my house again, Des. Not ever. You're not to so much as brush by another woman in the street. You see one of my girls, any girl for

239

that matter, out and about, you cross the road. You fail to do that and he'll be back here to pay you a more intimate visit. You understand me?'

Although Mahoney was in too much pain to reply, Viola was satisfied he'd got the message.

'And, Des. My bracelet?'

Mahoney pointed to his pants, lying on the floor. Viola went through the pockets and retrieved it. 'Thank you, Des.' She placed the bracelet around her wrist and admired it.

'On second thoughts, if I were you, I'd invest in insurance. Like moving. Interstate would be my suggestion.' She opened the door. 'I won't be seeing you again, Des. You take care of yourself and stay out of trouble.'

She walked back downstairs into the kitchen. The old man looked up at her, anxiously. She knew there was no need to bribe or threaten him to ensure he'd keep his mouth shut. Viola liked the newly arrived migrants from Europe. They worked hard, were polite to her girls when they visited the brothel and, best of all, they had an inherent quality for minding their own business.

'You married?' she asked him.

'No. My wife is dead. A daughter, I have.'

Viola took the diamond bracelet from her wrist and handed it to him. 'Be sure she gets this for her next birthday.'

Frank Slim was standing in the laneway. Viola took two envelopes from her handbag and handed the first one to him. 'That's for the work tonight. Two as we agreed.' She then handed him the second envelope. 'There's double in there. Four thousand. You hear of Mahoney misbehaving in future, pissing in the street, public littering, whatever it is, you be sure it's the last sin he commits. You need any more than that, you contact me through Johnny Circio.'

Frank took the envelope and felt its weight.

'I do trust you,' Viola added. 'The men I know that have any integrity, I can count on one hand with a couple of fingers to spare. You're one of them, Frank Slim.' She kissed him on the cheek and closed her handbag. 'I've scraped the shit from these streets off my shoes for the last time. I've a child to take care of.'

Moama

Bryan Andy

Bryan Andy is a Yorta Yorta man from Cummeragunja – an Aboriginal village on the Murray River. Bryan is a writer, radio broadcaster, theatre maker and art critic.

* **Moama** means 'place of the dead'

When I lived in Collingwood I started chatting to a guy on Grindr who was a few kilometres away. He told me he was watching a game of footy at the MCG. After weighing each other up and swapping pics, I invited him to my house and we had sex as the day's light faded and night crept in.

Between sex and small talk and lingering kisses, somewhere in the air he broke a long silence saying, 'It must be so much easier being accepted as Aboriginal with darker skin.' He told me he too was Aboriginal, that he was Wiradjuri, and in response to his original statement I said, 'Sometimes it is easier with darker skin, sometimes it isn't.'

The night soon settled in and, after checking his phone, he confessed he'd missed his train back to central Victoria. 'What, you think you're gonna stay here, do ya?' I asked him with a wry smile, tickling him before we both became a mess of uncontained giggles.

He spent the night with me in my bedroom. In my space with the photos of family on the wall, with my artefacts and artworks, my books and the items in my life that remind me of my home, Cummeragunja. He spent the night with me in my bed leaving his scent.

In the morning as I made him coffee, he fossicked through my books before picking up a rock that sat on a bookshelf. 'Is this ochre?' he asked, and I caught his eye and smiled. It was a smile that said: 'I'd forgotten or put aside that you're just like me, that you're Aboriginal with your light, freckled skin and sinewy limbs.' It was a smile of relief, a relief in knowing this Wiradjuri man who had pleased me, and honoured me, and slept in my arms, knew what the white rock was.

I explained that the ochre was from my home, my country. I told him how our white ochre is the most prized type because it is used for ceremony, and that it was a commodity in our culture, and that it still is. In my relief I told him he could have it, on the proviso that he look after it. He thanked me with a kiss, and took the ochre home with him that day to Dja Dja Wurrung country.

We continued to chat via Grindr and then via text. We expanded on our lives digitally: me in the city on Wurundjeri country; him in a regional town on Dja Dja Wurrung land.

We shared images, thoughts, jokes, insights, frustrations, dreams ... and we made arrangements to catch up. He'd let me know when he was visiting Melbourne, and I'd let him know that I was keen to see him. Sometimes he'd go see a football game at the 'G before joining me at my house; sometimes we'd eat out for lunch or dinner before going back to mine; sometimes we'd catch up for nothing else but sex – to hold each other, and marvel at each other's bodies, to become entangled in each other's hair, to smell and taste each other's skin.

One time, after planning via SMS to meet up, I waited for his train under the wavy roof of Southern Cross Station. I greeted him with a hug and a kiss, telling him that waiting for him on the platform made me feel like a wartime bride waiting for her soldier to return. We laughed at the heteronormativity of it as we left the platform, surrounded by people reuniting with their friends and loved ones, and others making their way into the thick of the city unaccompanied, alone.

That night we ate at an Italian restaurant, before I took him home where we fell into each other and fucked; we made love.

In the morning I made him coffee as he fossicked through my belongings, plucking books from the shelves, looking curiously at my photographs and paintings. As I passed him his coffee he reassured me he was looking after the rock of white ochre I gave him when we first met. Again I smiled with relief.

He left to catch a tram to the city – and that was the last time I saw him. That was the last time I ever heard from him.

I SMSed him a few weeks later to let him know I'd be heading home to Cummeragunja via Echuca, with a suggestion that we cross paths there, as he'd often talked about visiting that town, as his parents lived across the river in Moama.

He never responded to my text.

I went home to Cummeragunja to see my family and kept the sadness I felt about not seeing him to myself. I took his lack of response as a sign he was no longer interested in me. I wondered if he was in a relationship. Was I just an affair on the side? Maybe he was still in the closet …

Months passed and I continued to wonder about him and I took to social media to glean some insight into how he was. We weren't friends on Facebook, so I was left poring over the rare posts he'd made public, finding his charm and cheek in the quirky messages that populated his wall, messages about the footy, or Barbara Streisand or his longstanding crush on tennis player Andre Agassi. I figured he was out. I noticed his posts stopped around six months prior.

More time passed and I took to Google, entering his name and the town he lived in. The results were fruitless. I re-entered his name and wrote 'Moama' after his surname in the search bar. A PDF of a church newsletter showed up as the second result. I downloaded the file, opened it and found his name in the funeral notices with details of a church service being held in Echuca, followed by a burial at Moama Cemetery. He was listed as the beloved son of Jacinta and Ron.

There was no insight into how he died.

The following spring, when I was up home with my grandparents, I asked my grandfather how I might find a grave at the Moama Cemetery. In his life Pop has identified, marked and documented all of the graves at Cummeragunja, and I knew he'd give me an insight into how I might find the resting place of my lover and, thus, the confirmation that he had indeed passed.

Pop gave me his advice and I left him to continue working on a wooden cross he was making for the grave of one of his own friends.

That afternoon I wandered around the Moama Cemetery for almost an hour before I found his grave.

His gravestone reads like that of a person whose valued life has been cut short: his parents, his sisters, his brothers-in-law, and his many nephews are all named.

I cried as I removed the dry, brown ash leaves that were tangled in the ornaments placed on his grave – a small ceramic angel in perpetual, silent prayer; a vase filled with fake flowers;

and a fist-sized rock painted with blue, white, yellow and teal dots representing country. On the smooth rock was a trail of black kangaroo tracks passing a circle surrounded by three black figures, representing mob seated around a campfire. I held the rock in the palms of my hands lending it warmth before placing it back on his grave. I sat with him, staring at the portrait photo on his headstone, wondering about his long and sinewy limbs, his robust hair and the state of his utilitarian hands. I sat remembering the warmth and hunger of his kisses.

Still to this day I don't know how he died. It's a question that gnaws at me in a cycle of grief and relief, as I tell myself I'm doing a pretty good job, convincing myself that how he died is irrelevant or secondary to knowing he's no longer with us.

For years I carried hope for him like the heavy, dull weight of an empty coolaman. I've wondered about him, this Wiradjuri man who was once a nurse, who worked at the coalface in an emergency room, who has a mother and father who live on my country.

I've relived moments of shared passion, touching myself, consumed with thoughts of his body and lust, fuelled with memories of this Wiradjuri man who was a year younger than me, who helped me feel good and comfortable and complete in my skin.

I've carried love for this Wiradjuri man who was once my lover, this Wiradjuri man who was comfortable, confident and cheeky, and just like me he was gay and Aboriginal.

I've spent years trying to find comfort in knowing he's now at rest, six feet under, in the cream sand and white ochre embrace of my home, my country.

Notes on sources

Stories from this collection were first published in the following books and magazines, some of them as earlier versions:

Tara June Winch's 'Cloud Busting' was first published in *Swallow the Air*, University of Queensland Press, 2006.

Herb Wharton's 'Waltzing Matilda' was first published in *Where Ya' Been, Mate?*, University of Queensland Press, 1996.

Archie Weller's 'Shadows on the Wall' was first published in *Australian Short Stories*, issue 66, Pascoe Publishing, 2018.

Samuel Wagan Watson's 'The Release' was first published in *Westerly*, volume 64, issue 2, 2019.

Ellen van Neerven's 'Each City' was first published in *Kindred: Twelve queer #LoveOzYA anthology stories*, Walker Books, 2019.

Michael Torres's 'Rodeo Girl' was first published in *Northern Territory Literary Awards 2005*, Northern Territory Library, 2005.

Adam Thompson's 'Honey' was first published online at *Kill Your Darlings*, 9 July 2018.

Jared Thomas's 'The Healing Tree' was first published in *Meanjin*, volume 65, issue 1, 2006.

Alf Taylor's 'Wildflower Girl' was first published in *Westerly*, volume 54, issue 2, 2009.

Melanie Saward's 'Galah' was first published online at *Djed Press*, 3 November 2019.

Mykaela Saunders's 'River Story' was first published in *Australian Book Review*, August 2020.

SJ Norman's 'Stepmother' was first published online at *Kill Your Darlings*, 28 August 2017.

Cassie Lynch's 'Split' was first published in *Stories of Perth*, Seizure, 2018.

Melissa Lucashenko's 'Dreamers' was previously published in *The Best Australian Stories 2017*, Black Inc., 2017; and *The Near and the Far: New stories from the Asia-Pacific region*, Scribe, 2016. It also formed part of a public performance by Northern Rivers Performing Arts in Lismore in 2016.

Jeanine Leane's 'Forbidden Fruit' was previously published in *Ora Nui Special Edition: A collection of Maori and Aboriginal literature*, Anton Blank, 2013; and *The Canberra Times*, 2004.

Gayle Kennedy's 'The Golden Wedding Anniversary' was first published in *Me, Antman and Fleabag*, University of Queensland Press, 2007.

Jane Harrison's 'Born, Still' was first published in *Writing Black*, if:book Australia, 2014.

Tony Birch's 'Frank Slim' was first published in *Common People*, University of Queensland Press, 2017.

Bryan Andy's 'Moama' was originally presented as part of an evening of storytelling at the 2019 Blak & Bright Festival.

About the cover artist
Kukula Mcdonald

Skin name: Nampitjinpa
Language: Luritja
Date of birth: 28 September 1985
From: Uttumpatu
Community: Papunya, Northern Territory

Kukula Mcdonald is a Luritja woman from Papunya who has been painting at the Bindi Mwerre Anthurre Artists Studio since 2002. Kukula predominantly paints Red-Tailed Black Cockatoos and knows where to find 'big mobs' of them in the Central and Western Deserts. Kukula has become known for these Red-Tailed Black Cockatoos, which she incorporates into the landscape of Papunya, big mobs or a lone individual soaring in the sky. More recently, an occasional Yellow-Tailed Cockatoo, Galah or Ringneck parrot might make its way into Kukula's landscapes.

For more information, go to: bindiart.com.au/artist/kukula-mcdonald/

FIRE FRONT
Edited by Alison Whittaker

This important anthology, curated by Gomeroi poet and academic Alison Whittaker, showcases Australia's most-respected First Nations poets alongside some of the rising stars. Featured poets include Oodgeroo Noonuccal, Ruby Langford Ginibi, Ellen van Neerven, Tony Birch, Claire G. Coleman, Evelyn Araluen, Jack Davis, Kevin Gilbert, Lionel Fogarty, Sam Wagan Watson, Ali Cobby Eckermann, Archie Roach and Alexis Wright.

Divided into five thematic sections, each one is introduced by an essay from a leading Aboriginal writer and thinker – Bruce Pascoe, Ali Cobby Eckermann, Chelsea Bond, Evelyn Araluen and Steven Oliver – who reflects on the power of First Nations poetry with their own original contribution. This incredible book is a testament to the renaissance of First Nations poetry happening in Australia right now.

'A necessary and elaborate call to arms.' – *The Sydney Morning Herald*

'*Fire Front* celebrates both the established and emerging, the new and familiar. Each contribution is notable for its vivid, breathing compulsion. Together, they speak with – and toward – a living history.' – *Australian Book Review*

'*Fire Front* will always be relevant, at least for me (and maybe many First Nations readers like me) no matter what the year because of the Blak love and wisdom that exists within its pages. We will often have the desire to feel the strength of words it contains, like feeling the heat of a campfire on your face.' – *Cordite Poetry Review*

ISBN 978 0 7022 6272 2

THROAT
Ellen van Neerven

I am not aware of my power
you watch me build my weapon

Throat is the explosive second poetry collection from award-winning Mununjali Yugambeh writer Ellen van Neerven. Exploring love, language and land, van Neerven flexes their muscles and shines a light on Australia's unreconciled past and precarious present with humour and heart. Unsparing in its interrogation of colonial impulse, this book is fiercely loyal to voicing our truth and telling the stories that make us who we are.

'*Throat* is a brave and radical work. A work that deserves an equally radical and considered reading position. One that requires a suspension of western realism, history, temporality, literary conventions and values, binaries and expectations. Its potency leaves an aftertaste to savour as it lingers long.' – *Sydney Review of Books*

'A national poetic deliverance of what it means to be Aboriginal, proud and resilient - yesterday, today and tomorrow.' – Yvette Holt

'In this brilliant, witty collection, van Neerven puts a finger to the world's jagged pulse and measures out the beat across time and country, love and loss.' – Omar Sakr

'Van Neerven's ability to challenge and expand politics is thrilling, their flair for language exhilaratingly intimate.' – Nakkiah Lui

ISBN 978 0 7022 6291 3